for Ginny,

THREADS OF PASSION,

Joy and Peace

Fondly,

Holly.

THREADS OF PASSION

Holly Hayes

MUYBRIDGE PRESS

Published by Muybridge Press
1630 Sheridan Road, Wilmette, IL 60091
847-256-7500

07 06 05 04 03 ⌒ 5 4 3 2 1

This is a work of fiction. Names, characters, places, and incidents
either are the product of the author's imagination or are used fictitiously,
and any resemblance to actual persons, living or dead, events, or locales
is entirely coincidental.

PUBLISHER'S CATALOGING-IN-PUBLICATION DATA
Hayes, Holly.
Threads of passion / Holly Hayes.
p.   cm.
ISBN 0-9724555-0-7
Library of Congress Number: 2002112717
[1. Personality and emotions—Fiction. 2. Mood (Psychology)—Fiction.
3. Women—Mental health—Fiction. 4. Self-perception in women—
Fiction. 5. Seasons—Fiction. 6. Psychological fiction.] I. Title.
PS3608 .A947 P37   2003
813.6—dc21   CIP

Printed in the United States of America
Set in Weiss

For Carl

CONTENTS

THREADS OF PASSION

What we play is life.

~ LOUIS ARMSTRONG

WINTER

In dreams begins responsibility.

~ WILLIAM BUTLER YEATS

Merging with each wave that swelled beneath her breasts, Lexi surrendered to the warmth of the pulsing Caribbean Sea. Swimming always untangled her emotions. As she swam, her heart flooded with intense feelings, and she plucked them out—one at a time. Hopelessness, fear, then anger. But, she was safe in Barbados, far from yesterday's war zone, and felt secure enough in the pale tourmaline water to let locked-up feelings finally flow.

Parting the water with the slow, even rhythm of the breast-stroke, Lexi reclaimed herself. Gracefully, she extended her long arms, then breathed out as she pulled the water back toward her legs. Her head rose up for a second, then rested, as her legs completed the stroke. This was her second day in Barbados. She'd woken early this morning consumed by emotional chaos just thinking about Jake. Now the repetitious movements soothed her. Her heart outpaced her head. She started to tingle with new sensations.

If everyone got just one dream, hers would be the chance to retrieve her now dormant love of sensual pleasure. Passion would always be the crown jewel of the life she wanted to live. She needed to rejuvenate her sexuality to sustain herself—feed her creativity and refuel her energy. How else could she become the woman she'd hoped to be and find the happiness she fiercely sought?

That was the reason she had planned this vacation with her husband—to break the routine and turn the combustible energy between them from anger to passion. But in the end, Jake had bowed out, leaving Lexi ravaged by disappointment.

She remembered how her body and her spirit used to soar in the throes of ecstasy. It was the joy she'd first known in her twenties, when she'd happily left guilt and shame behind. She remembered uncharted expeditions into the ocean of pleasure that had been hers. Where had that brave soul gone?

The memory of such radiance gave her the courage to dive deep for her own sunken treasure. What she couldn't recall was when she'd lost it. Or the day she'd bartered it away for what, at the time, seemed more precious. Had her ambitions robbed her of ordinary pleasures? Is that when she traded balance for control? Or maybe she'd bargained herself away when she made those daily compromises with Jake, hoping in return that he'd take good care of her. Now, she was at a crossroads.

A prism of light drew her eyes toward the landscape below, and it was beautiful. A mirror image of its twin universe above ground, the land beneath the sea's surface teemed with plants and organisms. The ocean floor had its own social structure. It was a lot easier to see the wonder and the treasure in this simpler system. That's the kind of existence she wanted. She believed she could best grow and care for her sensuality by paring back her life and staying close to nature.

Lexi conjured up a habitat where balance reigned. She envisioned a world of lavish beauty, safe from the wrath of wind or water and stoked by a warming sun. Then she imagined the kind of man she'd take to such a glorious place. Her companion would be someone who loved her, understood passion, and led with kindness.

Theirs would be a life of sensual pleasure. Tender glances, warm squeezes, plus that elusive, eternal torch they'd carry for one another. Together, they'd create a sex life far better than anything in the movies. For her, that was the crazy glue of a relationship. That was her basis for building a family that would stay together. The fantasy underscored the failure of her marriage.

Like the healing caduceus with two snakes wrapped tight around Hermes' winged staff, the crazy glue she and the right lover could manufacture would weld them together, unleash her wildest desires, then bring her back to center. She imagined love's infinity as a process of losing herself in order to find herself. And him. The truest love would be an extraordinary connection won through surrender in order to discover something neither had known before. Over time they'd satisfy their longings by building bridges between their imaginations. Fascinated by interlocking fantasies, they'd grow together. Always together.

Lexi turned over, needing the full support of the sea. Floating on her back, she took in a deep breath, then eased into a soothing, rhythmic pattern. She stretched out, hands behind her head. Looking up at the sky for a while, she closed her eyes and let her eyelids absorb the radiance of the sun's afterimage. She let the light roam down her chest to her belly. Luminous around her pelvis, it hovered for a while, and reassured her that her sexual feelings were very close to the skin. The sun's touch played upon her body's automatic responses and she was wet now, not only on the outside.

For Lexi, the sun beating down on her with such affection was a premonition. Perhaps the essence of her dream was the need to turn herself into a well-loved golden orb. Her body was telling her that she needed to love herself, as tenderly and passionately as the bright gold Barbadian sun was loving her right now.

More hopeful, she let the gentle waves bring her close to the shore. Once there, she stood in the shallow water and wiggled her toes into the wet sand. Barbados was a smorgasbord of pleasures. And in its midst, it was easy to believe there were more than just five senses. Looking toward the horizon, she lost herself in a sunset that was just starting to form. A sheer cirrus film, invisible by day, turned light pink around the edges of the sun. As the sun began its patient descent into the ocean, she watched the color change. The golden blaze of day softened. Taking on a redder cast, the hues changed both subtly and immediately, much like a blushing woman. In time, it would be on fire.

Drinking in the beauty, she turned slowly back toward the beach and walked toward the water's edge. The waves rushed around her ankles like eager new friends wanting to take her somewhere. And at about the height of her shoulders, yet miles away, the power of the setting sun urged her forward.

Broad and sturdy, yet soft to the eye, Lexi's shoulders defined her presence. They were an asset in spaghetti straps or strapless garb, and she used them to full advantage. They did more than make her hips look smaller by comparison. In business, her shoulders put her on par with men. Squaring up with someone taller or filling out a leather office chair, Lexi took up enough space to be taken seriously. Sometimes that could be a burden.

She'd been given much responsibility. Plus impossible dead-lines.

But even her shoulders felt better now. Massaged by the sun, her shoulders had loosened after only two idle days. They moved easily from side to side in sync with the rush of water at her feet. Were those broad shoulders still in charge, or were they, too, on holiday, following her body rather than leading, taking on the natural sway of her hips? She was moving fluidly now. She felt giddy, even intoxicated, by her body and its rhythm.

Struck by the delicious movement, Lexi wondered how she'd ever let herself stray from such grace. In fact, she rarely cele-brated any of her physical features. She'd been sort of practical about it all. Her five-feet, eight-inch frame served her well. She was erect, even energetic, and that was sufficient. Yet she had one ploy to celebrate her body: she always looked for her ideal weight under the large-frame column of any weight chart. On paper, she'd always be thin.

Her frame was more than a good pedestal for her face. Her wide-set, sea-foam green eyes looked huge on an oval face. Full lips, more classical than bee-stung, added beauty, she'd been told, and promised a generous spirit. Her smile, though, was what lit up her face. Wide and moist, she unleashed its charm as she walked down the beach alone. She felt natural and alive. She was at peace and pursed her lips as she moved closer to the resort, wondering what would happen next.

Winding around the scarlet hibiscus bush at the corner of Sandy Lane's Beach Club, Lexi saw Steven, a waiter, setting the tables for dinner. She'd been aroused by him at breakfast, enjoy-ing the feeling. They'd interacted so naturally in the morning light, enjoying each other's glances and subtle movements. In the twilight, he did a slow dance, not minding the repetition of placing forks, knives, and spoons in the right spots. She knew this was why Barbados intrigued her. It was the beauty of the people. Were they alone awakening her desire?

"Hello, Steven," she said warmly, feasting on his dark, kind face. Her heart reached out to him, ready to caress all that she could see. She loved the drama of the big brown eyes that swung toward her from deep, white sockets. She felt like a woman in his presence.

"Well, good evening, Mrs. Lankford." His soft, slightly accented voice was as delicate as the native flora and fauna. His lips mirrored his eyes. Like perfectly choreographed lovers on one face, both parts moved together. She fixated on his soft, giving lips. His face was a mix of light and dark. The ruby lips looked vulnerable hiding in the shadows of his brown skin. They were rimmed with skin as colorful as an Italian blood orange. In motion, his lips were a prelude to passion.

"The ocean is perfect today," she said, turning her body at a slight angle to his.

"You sure look relaxed now," he laughed, ever so slowly mirroring her stance and giving her the encouragement she needed.

"Your smile this morning helped. That's how you must make all the guests feel, Steven. I'm learning a lot about seeing beauty wherever I look in Barbados," she said with spirit.

"Enjoy your evening," he replied, much like a father whose eyes light up knowing that good things are in store for his daughter. Big wide eyes of love.

"You, too," she said, sensing that he enjoyed the moment as much as she did.

As she took the path to her room, she thought more about Steven's presence. His inner beauty. As the first stop on the slave trade, Barbados had been populated by the biggest, healthiest, and most able Africans to be kidnapped from the continent.

Barbados had mystique. It started with its name. Barbados. All those vowels bracketed by b's and d's were reminiscent of the leisurely pace of an afternoon devoted to love.

But the sensual beauty was making her ache. All day long she swam and walked amidst it. The lush scenery brightened her mood. As dusk fell, Lexi felt a pang. It had been a long time since her body projected the sensual vitality of Steven's. She was parched from a relationship that had lost its moisture long ago. Lexi's mantra-for better or for worse-had been more soothing when Jake's black moods were intermittent. Now Jake's resentment seemed to grow in direct proportion to her success. As his attacks on her became personal, her patience waned. Some days she felt like no more than a ghost of a woman.

Her life was a series of deadlines. While meeting each one was gratifying, the pattern was scary. Could work alone create the rich texture of the life she wanted? Blessed with good health, she sensed her journey would be a long one. Lexi had always known that she could best develop her soul through relationships. She believed that building connections to others, particularly one significant other, was the most important task in her life. Marriage was the starting point.

Just twenty-eight years old, Lexi knew that she deserved something better than the sawtooth pattern of her life. Once she became clear about her own needs, trying harder to make Jake happy, as her mother suggested, mattered less. Taught to believe that the give-and-take between partners was what held a marriage together, she had growing doubts about their relationship. Up to now she had been afraid to take big risks, the kind that would let Jake know when enough was enough.

This new dream assumed she'd separate herself from what

she naively believed she'd promised at the altar—fidelity to one man, and to be happy with that forever after. She wondered how things between herself and Jake had deteriorated to the point where she would throw it all away looking for a fantasy lover.

What if the connection she imagined was not a total fantasy? Perhaps she could find a lover who would share her passion. One with whom she'd create a new reality. Someone who respected her. Suddenly Lexi felt exhausted, depleted, confused.

Opening the door to her room, she wanted to fling herself on the bed and have a good cry. Why tease herself with unattainable dreams? There was no safe haven in her life for such luxurious fantasies. No prospect for crazy glue.

But Barbados was not a place to wallow. It was a lush island— one that bred opportunities to heal her damaged senses. Willing to explore her dream, she was eager to be among other people. She would take the hotel's evening trip into town, joining other tourists for a cocktail cruise on the *Sea Goddess*, a local tourist attraction.

Summoning up the spunk to create a new look, she experimented. Wispy images of pale chiffon crossed her mind. Then the bold contrast of red and black. Pants that cut a striking silhouette rivaled notions of a softer, more feminine style. Used to standing out—for better or for worse—in a world of minimal fashion, she enjoyed adding an elaborate accessory to each outfit. She tried flowing scarves and the few pieces of elegant jewelry that she traveled with to flesh out different looks.

Lexi wanted to be as spectacular as her surroundings. Captivated by the beauty of the beach, she hoped to appear just as sensual. Color. Sure, she loved it—particularly red. But right now she wanted to create an earthy look, like the broad, green, waxy leaves on the island that merged with yards and yards of dense, flowering hedges.

Feeling a bit awkward, Lexi pulled a black spandex tube top over her firm, naked breasts, high enough on her chest to hold their own. In the mirror, she saw that her bosom looked as natural as the curves on the beach. The silhouette of her image made her less angry at Jake. His absence gave her time to learn something new about herself, and it felt great.

Running the soft, rich cotton of her rain-forest-green sarong through her hands, she practiced kneading two thick cords of fabric while she watched in the mirror. When they were just right, she gave them a big squeeze. Hoping to remember how to tie these things, she slid the material back and forth across her hips, settling it off-center a bit. Then she pulled the cords together into a knot. With the split in the fabric positioned toward the front, she looked casual yet chic.

To set off her eyes, she searched for the thin strand of fresh-water pearls she'd tossed in at the last minute. Just in case the resort was fancier than she'd expected. Hesitating as she plucked them from her jewelry pouch, Lexi was pleased to notice how the delicate, white shapes popped against her cinnamon brown throat. She nodded to herself in the mirror. Not bad for just two days in the sun.

Swaying gracefully back and forth as she summoned up the look, Lexi felt confident. And electric with desire for all the vitality denied her. Was she, like a jazz artist, starting to play from the inside out? The thought reminded her of her father, dead now for a few years. He had loved jazz and had taught her an appreciation for Louis Armstrong, Duke Ellington, and Miles Davis, as well as Brubeck. She remembered how they'd listened to tunes together, tapping them out on furniture or an available knee, with fingers or a pen. That's when he said they were playing from the inside out. Just the way the pros did. Giving both nipples a quick nip, she arched her back and flicked off the lights.

All done up and laughing out loud, she walked to the hotel lobby. As she pinched a hibiscus flower off a bush and nestled it behind her left ear, she wondered who would ever believe that her romantic Caribbean retreat for two could boil down to taking outings in vans with droves of strangers. And that she was dressing as though she were meeting someone with a lotus heart. She flung herself into the experience and hoped for the best.

Struck by how natural it felt to head off to a social gathering on her own, Lexi wondered what had changed. Was it the sun or the lush surroundings that put her in touch with her needs? Or anger that had loosened, then cracked? No matter, she felt freer, inside and out, able to unleash her passion, which had been buried of late. And she could almost hear her mother ask, "What in your heart of hearts, Alexis Lankford, do you now *know?*" How could she ever tell Jake enough is enough?

Her heavy thoughts lifted as she hoisted herself into the resort van, already filled with a half-dozen couples, and tucked in by the window of the broad bench seat in the back. Two younger women followed. When the first one saw her, she gave a quick look back to her companion, who, in turn, gave her a nod. They slid over, almost in one motion.

"Hi, I'm Sabrina Mueller," said the slender, dark-haired woman as she extended her hand. "We noticed you yesterday when we arrived. You looked so relaxed. It made us glad to be here."

"I'm Lexi Lankford," she said, smiling appreciatively. "Time alone can do that. How long will you be here?"

"A week. Amy Karan," said the other woman, as she reached over to shake hands. She was probably Lexi's age though she looked older, sunken in some way—perhaps depressed.

Not minding that they had wrested her from her thoughts, Lexi felt like sharing her burden. "Had expected to be here with my husband," Lexi said. "But he couldn't make it. His work. I'm exhausted. Figured I could read and sunbathe alone."

"That's all I want to do," said Amy.

Sabrina raised an eyebrow in mock dismay. "Well, I'd love to meet someone terrific," she said wryly, tilting her head toward Amy as she talked to Lexi. "I haven't been in a steady relationship for over a year, and I can't figure out why."

"My husband and I split up last fall," said Amy.

Lexi sensed Amy's pain as she spoke quickly, then pulled back. So she, too, was here to restore herself.

Going deeper into her own dilemma, Lexi felt oddly safe in the midst of strangers. Safe enough to burst. "I wish I knew what I wanted. Other than a salve for disappointment." Lexi spoke from her heart. "Maybe something exotic. As wild as this flower," gesturing to the blossom tucked behind her ear.

They all laughed, and when the van hit the last pothole, Sabrina leaned forward and said, "Go for it."

They spoke freely, three women who might never see each other again, sharing an unusual intimacy. As they lowered themselves from the van, quick smiles were all they had left to share. Each in pursuit of some healing, they disbanded.

Lexi turned to the chartered vessel. Struck by its beauty, she let others pass while she paused to take a closer look. It was a schooner with white sails lashed to its twin masts. The boat had grace and mystery well beyond its size. The *Sea Goddess* was the kind of craft that could have sailed straight out of a Grace Kelly movie.

Eager to go aboard, Lexi crossed the gangplank. A stocky seaman greeted her, swiveling a large tray filled with drinks on the fingers of one hand.

"A rum punch?" he asked. "We're celebrating tonight. You know, we Barbadians invented rum."

As he moved the tray closer to her, the sailor flexed his bicep muscle, and the navy stripes on his nautical jersey wiggled. "Pardon my boldness," he continued, "but you won't want to miss this."

Lexi picked up cup of the deep red island punch and toasted him. "I don't want to miss anything on this trip. Thanks."

"We're an island of plenty, that's for sure," he said, as he turned to greet the guest behind her.

Lexi stopped short as she caught sight of a tall, rugged man. His long, sculpted face, chiseled out around the eyes, held a mystery she wanted to unravel. Curly brown hair, a few shades darker than the day-old beard, looked earthy against his golden skin. A dark tan made it tough to guess his age. Thin, long lips balanced out his cheeks' asymmetrical lines. He was handsome in the daring way that had attracted her to 'bad boys' when she was younger.

Her pulse quickened as she watched how he maneuvered his hard body. Lexi yearned to give in to the magnetism of his dark, marine-blue eyes. Watching him closely as he moved easily between jocular conversation with the crew and greetings to the guests, Lexi decided he must be the man in charge.

Their eyes met more than once as the group's pace speeded up with the discovery of a bar on the boat's lower deck. The crowd churned, forming conversational groups, round and round, up and down the boat's pathways. Lexi dared to stop not far from where the tawny stranger stood at the captain's wheel. She felt an uneasy attraction, then stilled herself. Was it the fancy of her own imagination that lured her, the hopeful antic-ipation of adventure? Or did the pull he had for her suggest a deeper connection?

He took a step forward and tilted his head down to about the height of her eyes. With a penetrating look, he let his blue eyes roam her face. His nostrils widened as his chest expanded, just before he greeted her in rich, sonorous tones, which came from deep within his torso.

His words were as simple as his presence was complex. "Hello. I'm Ross, your host."

Lexi's eyes flickered as her lips moved cautiously into a smile. "Quite a ship you've got here," she said, softening her knees for better support on the deck. It was as though she could feel the waves swell under the floorboards and then come up between her toes.

"She serves me well," he said, twisting to the side to duck the rays of the setting sun. Then he slowly rubbed his thigh and in one slick move, pushed his hand down over his jeans.

"Is that what you like?" she asked boldly. Lexi instinctively ran her fingers through her hair.

"We work hard to please," he said, eyes softening as he steadied them on hers.

With a quick jolt of her head, Lexi said, "That's what makes the difference." Taunting him with her eyes, then teasing with her shoulders, she swiveled toward him.

"Makes it memorable," Ross said, coughing throatily.

"I don't doubt that," Lexi said, feeling as though she'd already surrendered.

"How long are you here, my pretty?" he asked, looking as if he needed to ground her now.

"A few more days," she said slowly.

"With girlfriends?" he wondered, as his hand slid across his temple, smoothing the curly locks.

"No. Alone this trip," she said, then straightened up and pressed her shoulders back slightly to center herself.

His words seemed unnecessary, as a wide smile stretched across his face. "Sounds good to me. Everybody needs it."

In almost the same beat, her eyes moved slowly up toward his and she said, "Some more than others."

"Would you like to get together?" Ross asked, as he moved his tongue to the corner of his mouth.

"Okay," she said softly, then lightning hit her innards, burning a jagged path from her belly to her temple.

The sides of his mouth turned up as he took another step forward. Using his softest tones yet, he tilted his head slightly. "Where shall I call you?"

"Sandy Lane," she said, alarmed that the mirage she had conjured up just this afternoon was materializing. "Lexi Lankford."

His lips and eyes registered a deep satisfaction. "I'm having the strangest sensation," he whispered as his fingers brushed against his starched white shirt. "Like an earthquake starting up." And after a long silence he said, "Till then. The hardest part will be the wait."

Lexi's eyes widened. Weightless, she paused to find sure footing as she turned to leave. The passage from the boat back to the group was a blur. Gripping the seat of the van, she settled herself down, just as Sabrina and Amy climbed aboard.

"Nice going," Sabrina said. "We saw him, too. But you got there first."

"Very attractive," Lexi said, resisting the urge to comfort Sabrina. Then flippantly added, "Nothing I can't handle, though," as she wondered if she were really that secure.

"How about you?" Lexi asked Amy. The young woman looked even more downcast than before. Lexi had the urge to reach out and stroke her, to help ease her pain.

"Amy could have gotten lucky," Sabrina spoke for her friend. "She was chatted up all evening by an interesting guy from

Chicago. A commodities trader. Pass him on to me if you're not interested," Sabrina said matter-of-factly, turning to her quiet friend.

Lexi intervened. "When I told my best friend about the trip, she said, "If you really want something to change, it will." In fact, these had been Shakti's parting words at the airport.

Sabrina said, "I need more to go on than that. Any maps?"

"Well, Shakti says it has to do with our intentions."

"I think she's right," Amy said softly, as the van pulled into Sandy Lane.

A tasteful, even beautiful spot, the luxury resort felt alive from the inside out. Lexi went directly to the dining area. She loved this spot, its tables contained within a white-tented pavilion, where a wooden floor had been extended out to the beach. The pavilion was so close to the ocean she felt she was back on the boat's deck.

Lexi's eyes panned the large space. The other guests were arriving in dribs and drabs, taking their places at family-style tables. Clusters of votive candles on the tables threw flames that danced against the crests of the waves, that broke just yards from the tent. The décor was all white—chairs, tablecloths, and orchids—and created a celestial feel. The whole pavilion seemed a part of the water and the sky.

Lexi sat down and basked in the delicacy of the Ravi Shankar recording that Jake would have hated. And actively, at that. He'd dismiss it as odd, insubstantial. Being alone helped her understand the real appeal of the music. What she treasured was the space between the notes. She had worried that Jake's negative dialogue would follow her to Barbados. But she was free of it.

The table swelled with oversized white plates full of Caribbean barbecue, curried goat, fish simmered in coconut milk, and pigeon peas, garnished with red tomatoes. Lexi's favorite was coo-koo pudding, a traditional medley of sweet potato, pumpkin, and onion. Running the purée around her tongue, she could taste the anise, and the ginger had a bite to it.

The chic, dark-haired French woman Lexi had noticed last night was seated across from her at the table for eight. Marguerite could be thirty or fifty. Her style and élan made it impossible to put her in any category at all. Another benefit of traveling alone—one was forced to reach out for company. "It's hard to know if it's the spice or the texture that make this so incredible," Lexi said, gesturing to her plate and wondering if her enthusiasm was triggered more by her encounter with Ross.

"In France, we say the taste is as much a measure of the shopping as the cooking," said Marguerite, as she straightened her torso.

"Really?" Lexi replied, picturing Marguerite moving briskly through French markets.

"But of course. Everything must be fresh. That's when it's beautiful. Like swiss chard. The red veins running through thick leaves. All because of the firm, ruby stems," Marguerite said, running her hand up an imaginary stalk.

Lexi thought again of Ross. "I love eggplant," Lexi said. "I always look for a deep, purply one. Then hold it in my palm, and squeeze. It's mine if it's firm and heavy." Smiling, Lexi enjoyed the image.

"Absolutely. Plenty of juice," Marguerite said, as if she understood completely.

"I buy corn after the Fourth of July," Lexi continued, eager to keep the sensual metaphor alive. "I flick the hairs at the top of the cob. If they're silky, I gently open the husk. When I press down at the base of a kernel, I know it's sweet if juice flows."

Don, the American next to Lexi, was clearly waiting for an opening in the conversation. He said, "I like chocolate mousse. What about that?"

"Oh, chocolate," Lexi said in a mock sultry voice and noticed Marguerite smiling. "The cocoa bean is extraordinarily sensitive. I've heard that the best ones come from St. Lucia, not far from here. They're hand-picked, you know. Some say the women in St. Lucia have the softest hands in the Caribbean."

Don laughed, looked at his wife, and said, "And I thought I fell for you because of your cooking. Maybe it was your hands."

"Hands are important," Lexi teased. "But a man who cooks could easily find his way to my heart."

Jacques, so elegant in a white linen shirt, said, "Marguerite and I cook together. That's even better."

"I think you're right," Lexi said, slowly, savoring the idea.

Feeling buoyant when she left the table, Lexi hoped to find the message light on when she returned to her room, but was disappointed. She wondered if Ross had been genuine. Perhaps he had just been doing his job—entertaining the lonely ladies. Making them feel attractive. Getting their blood running hot enough to flirt with a safer crowd back at the resort. Her heart pounded and the nakedness scared her. Lexi felt vulnerable. Her banter with Ross had made her feel bright and courageous. Her fantasy had seemed close at hand. She couldn't afford to lose it, any of it. She'd uncovered her long lost desire today and needed to dig her sex life out of the black hole that had contained it for so long.

Lexi couldn't go backward. Hoping for some clarity, she was sorting through notions of what to do next when the phone rang.

"Hello."

"Lexi, this is Ross. We're just finishing up. I was hoping to stop over tonight, but it's getting late. Are you free tomorrow night?"

"Tomorrow would be great," she said. She didn't feel shy about letting her excitement show.

Either the mystique of Barbados or her time spent soul-searching had stripped away more formal decorum. Lexi was closer to the primal urges that she'd put away somewhere down the road. Was marriage the opposite of freedom, or was it specifically her marriage to Jake?

Enough of that. The date set, Lexi had a world of things to consider.

Morning brought a rare enthusiasm for the day. The birds that hovered around the patio breakfast table echoed her sense of freedom. With more energy than she usually had at this hour, Lexi jotted a quick postcard to Shakti, her closest friend and best ego booster.

In college, she and Shakti made a pact to become the kind of women who lived from passion. Shakti thought of it as her birthright, something tied up with her core beliefs. She oriented her life according to dharma. Lexi understood that it was Shakti's belief that each person had a special talent that was to be used in the service of others.

For Lexi, at eighteen, that notion was a newfound creed, and it grew to have the resonance of a dream. Passion mattered in both work and love. Shakti said that once Lexi discovered her purpose, success would depend on how fully she lived from her essence. Shakti also believed that it was easy to love a man. It was like harnessing the harmony and joy of the universe. Lexi must have looked confused, because that was when Shakti said that together, she and Lexi would learn to grow like the lotus. A metaphor for the human heart, the lotus held the promise of the universe tucked inside its petals. Everything seemed possible.

As she put the postcard back in her purse and left the table, Lexi knew the day was bound to be a celebration of possibilities. The pleasures washed over her. Eager for her morning walk, the highlight of each day she'd been here, she lathered herself with oil, tucked her shoulder-length hair into a cap, and slid a pair of Vuarnet sunglasses over her temples. As she headed toward the beach, her eyes fixed on the line where the water and sky met. Blue on blue. Mist and reflection coming together. Looking out to the horizon gave her a new way of being.

Unafraid of moving toward her dream, she headed into the surf to wash the sunscreen off her hands and felt open to the changes she'd set in motion. The tepid water tickled as it swirled around her legs. In and out. Side to side. The remnants of the small waves stretched as far as possible toward the dunes, then receded, a constant flow. Waves lapped over each other. Lots of patterns. Lots of prospects.

The narrow, palm-lined beach looked endless, with serpentine twists that promised adventure. Just how far might she go? Today everything on the beach held a new fascination. The sand had more luster. The ocean seemed more animated, waves along the shoreline gyrated back and forth, as if to a reggae beat.

Even the beach's curves seemed more sensuous and mysterious than yesterday. Hawkers of bikinis and sarongs peddled garb designed to make the human form seductive. Whatever senses the sea, the sand, and the sky didn't stimulate, the beach trade could. Massages and hair plaiting piggybacked on parasailing and outrigger rentals. Small businesses were fanning out—a commingling of services designed to serve the body and soothe the mind. A walk down the beach brought enough stimulation to touch a hundred acupressure points in myriad ways. Filling up stomachs was not Barbados's only attraction.

Lexi gravitated toward the native vendors. A woman with milk-chocolate eyes that sparkled approached her and wanted to braid her hair.

"Yes," Lexi said without hesitation, "I'd like that." For such intimate contact Lexi felt it important they exchange names. "By the way, I'm Lexi."

"Mari," the woman said with a tentative smile.

They sat a couple of hundred feet in from the ocean, beneath a tree. The warmth of the sand on Lexi's thighs and bottom triggered thoughts of the evening to come.

"How pretty," she smiled, studying the beads that would set off her braids, "I like the red ones."

Mari moved in close to Lexi and knelt at her side. The rounded cheeks of the beachside beautician stayed still while her capable, sinewy hands set a rapid pace. She combed Lexi's thick, wavy hair slowly. With even pressure, she massaged Lexi's scalp as she parted her curls. Dividing the honey-blonde locks into sections, she'd periodically rest and smooth the parcels along the way, developing the design as she worked. The interludes were an important part of the experience's luxury.

Having someone comb her hair felt good. It was a vacation in itself. Lexi was happy to shed the responsibility—the strokes, the care, and the master plan. It was like all the repetitive tasks she did for herself every morning, but now there was someone to help her.

Lexi considered starting up a conversation, but instead let her breathing slow while she watched a group of children building sand castles. All in perpetual motion. Some were digging. Others building. And intermittently, each one ran back and forth to the ocean with a bucket, eager to fortify the castle with the weight of wet sand. Their excited squeals and chatter stoked Lexi's soul.

Skillfully, the agile woman with the age-lined hands made her way through the neat furrows of Lexi's hair. Her hands danced as she drew the hair up and out. First a quick, taut pull of the locks. Then, after separating them into threes, she moved the strands back and forth, back and forth, braiding with the rhythm of a basket weaver. As each wooden bead finished off an end, Lexi could feel the importance of the work build.

Mari came around in front of Lexi when she was done and gave her a beautiful smile. Mari's luminous eyes relayed the same warmth that flowed from her caring hands. Lexi lifted herself from the sandy spot. After Lexi paid her, she reached for Mari's hand and held it affectionately.

Lexi then headed down the beach with her plaited hair swinging from side to side like some sort of musical accompaniment. The flip flop of her braids made her laugh. Certain that she looked as magnificent on the outside as she felt inside, Lexi was aglow. A rush of new feelings simultaneously connected her to the island and to the world in a more powerful and complete way.

After lunch Lexi decided to indulge in a siesta on her patio. Feeling simultaneously serene and energetic, she wiggled around the chaise until she located the part that sagged slightly, hoping for some cocoon-like comfort. The sun trickled through the branches overhead, depending on the breeze. She read and dozed.

An hour later, Lexi sat up with a start, hoping to catch her dream, but it darted away as soon as she moved. This was a good time to call Jake and see how his writing was going. He might feel less pressured, as she did, with this time alone. Perhaps they would have a good connection. In which case, did that mean her fantasy would be null and void?

Back in her room she phoned him. "Hi, sweetheart." She tried to put sincerity into her voice, hoping that acting with warmth toward him might rouse some extra feeling in herself.

"Well, well," Jake said, his cynical tone registering the tension he felt whenever Lexi went away. "How's the Queen of the Caribbean?"

"She's pretty good," Lexi countered, willing to get into combat mode if necessary. "As a matter-of-fact, I was just thinking how much you'd like this place."

"That is, if I could like anything now, huh?"

"That's not what I said."

"No. It's what I said."

"What's up?"

"Another hole in the research. More turgid prose. And a bunch of assholes who are supposed to be my colleagues."

"One of those days, huh?"

"Cut the crap, Lexi. They're all that way! You're the big shot. I play houseboy."

"Is that right? What about wanting to be more than your alcoholic father?"

"And you? Do you miss your killer colleagues? Those intellectual giants."

"If that was supposed to be funny, I'm not laughing." She was astonished at how they could go from 'hello' to 'go to hell' in record time.

"Okay, okay. I got a little hot. I'm just in a lousy mood."

"Sorry. Thought being alone might give you some space."

"Probably not enough. You left me here with me, you know."

"You'll do fine. You just need more time. Are you sleeping much?"

"No more than usual."

"That's too bad."

"Yep. It bites."

"Well, if it's any consolation, I'm going to work a bit myself this afternoon. I promised to review the financials of a company that's invented an interactive TV." Lexi helped Bradford Communications buy and build the earnings of high growth companies.

"Thanks for calling, Lexi. I really mean that."

And he did mean it. She knew that. But concern for each other did not stop the frustration she felt at the level of discomfort between them. "Yep. Feel better. Love you."

"You, too."

"Bye."

No better. No worse. Just more of the same. Louis, her closest male friend, always said, "The long run is a series of short run curves." Lexi worked very closely with Louis and depended on his sense of humor to negotiate through the often surreal meetings with their CEO. He was sort of a Geiger counter for her emotions. After a short conversation with Louis, she always knew when she had issues to address.

Right now, she sensed she was moving closer to some truth and wanted a better look at all the pieces. Louis was right. Life was a series of episodes. So why did hers seem to be one long rerun? Was she flunking Life 101 or what? To block out her anxiety, Lexi grabbed her briefcase, hoping to shed the conversation with Jake as she delved into her work.

Lexi grew sleepy as her mixed-up feelings kept intruding on her work. She needed to retreat to a part of herself that could sort the seeds. Breathing smoothly and from the diaphragm, she imagined herself back in the ocean. Caressed by the rhythm of the waves, she relaxed. She felt sexual as she gently moved her body and imagined making passionate love. The image vanished as she opened her eyes, feeling queasy.

In her heart of hearts, Lexi knew she and Jake had stopped

loving each other. What she didn't know was what to do about it. She decided to call Shakti for help, despite the expense. Shakti had wisdom well beyond her twenty-eight years. Shakti also spoke with more certainty than Lexi, which she valued when confused. Lexi imagined that Shakti's words were supported by thousands of years of Indian beliefs, and they grounded her.

Buoyed by hearing Shakti's voice, Lexi blurted out that she wanted to leave Jake. Shakti interrupted her.

"You have to work it out," said Shakti.

"I'm sick of it all. Just sick to death."

"You're married. It's your job."

"My job is to grow like the lotus, remember? And to be happy."

"Have you forgotten that the lotus grows in water? For us that means emotions, even painful ones. The roots of the lotus anchor it. How else could it survive monsoons? And those same roots, jutting straight down in the water, feed it—even under a scorching sun."

"Well, I'm parched, all right."

"Lexi, are you really following your passion? Jake's always supported that."

"I need to feel passion in both work and love. The problem is we're growing at different rates, and he's breaking the promise. He's closing me out—me and the rest of the world. And now I know the difference between pain and agony."

"If you are telling me this because you want me to say it's okay for you to leave him, I won't. It's not."

"I'm not Hindu. I'm not even Catholic."

"You have a responsibility to him. More to the point, you'd slow your spiritual growth."

"Is my responsibility to him or to me?"

"It is to God."

"God wants us to grow. When we're growing, God is happy."

"There is more."

Lexi felt like sobbing. Hadn't she tried everything she knew how to do? Maybe Shakti was made of something stronger. Something that Lexi didn't know how to access. Did she have the courage to try one more time?

"You're so good to me," Lexi whispered.

"And why not?"

"No. Really. To listen to all this negative stuff."

"Lexi, just six months ago you saved Ravi's life."

"That was easy. All I did was pick him up and notice he had trouble breathing."

"And I was a thousand miles away, and wouldn't have been home for three more days."

"So I took him to the doctor. Anyone would have done that."

"You may recall I was paying over one hundred dollars a day to someone who didn't."

"My instincts are better."

"The doctor said he wouldn't have made it through another day."

"Nobody knew how dangerous that virus was."

"You did."

"It was a hunch. Like now."

"You can always cut through everything. This is why I love you. And why I'm glad you have some time alone."

"But I'm scared I can't handle it."

"Can't take a journey inward?"

"Well, maybe. It's like Eden here."

"Careful, Lex."

Lexi's hand quivered as she eased the phone back on its base. Shakti had taken her through her paces, and she was surprised by the way she had fought back. She had never mentioned the date with Ross. They did agree, though, about the value of being alone, as difficult as that seemed now.

Perhaps taking a warm bath would soothe her. Gathering her bath products together she drew the water. The set was a gift from her mother, who'd taught her that small luxuries often outshine more expensive ones. Breathing the eucalyptus scent into her lungs as she lowered herself into the tub, Lexi finished her preparations and shook bubble mixture into the tub before turning off the faucet. Sloshing the water from side to side, then around and around, she felt safe, caught in a net of bubbles. The soapy luster made her buoyant. She felt much the way she did in the ocean. There was a sense of wellness to it all. All of her femininity was exposed and on the surface.

She ran her hands down the sides of her body, noting the soft slickness of the lubricants she'd added to the tub. Sinking down, she enjoyed the fine line between balance and loss of control. As she flirted with images of her evening, she ran her hand around her breasts, again and again, in a figure-eight motion. Yes, she was satisfied with their size and shape. Like breadfruit, the legendary South American food that people believed could feed an entire continent, her breasts had enough mass to sway gently when she walked. She relished her earth-mother state of mind and twisted her body, letting the oblong mounds of fruit make ripples in the water.

Her breasts were luminous in contrast to the tan lines that darkened her torso. They were a milk-bottle white, like a pair of large moonstone drop earrings she'd bought from a vendor at the beach. With her knees propped up and drifting toward the sides of the tub, she stroked her pelvis gently, then played with her hair that floated like Japanese seaweed.

Her labia began to swell with excitement. In her imagination her inside passage added to the water the most beautiful specimen of all. Pushing her whole pelvis up into her hand, she was eager for the attention. Deeper and deeper her fingers went on their dive for treasure. As she spread open her petals with the fingers on her left hand, she uncovered her essence with her right. Slowly, gently, she circled her clitoris. Then brushed it lightly. Staccato taps gave way to even pressure. She trusted herself completely and knew her dream was starting to unfold.

Alone in her porcelain cradle, she freed herself with an orgasmic laugh. A sound she remembered from college days. One that came from her heart—from a wellspring of love that was meant for sharing. As the quickening inside her waned, Lexi touched her flushed checks, now hotter than the water. Happy to have built a bridge between her desires and Ross, a man who might be able to help her reap them, Lexi rested before figuring out what to wear.

As Lexi dressed, she conjured up an image of the moment when Ross would strip her bare. Why not dress simply to ease the awkward moment of undressing? A gold band latched the top of a red silk halter around her neck. The fabric swept gently across her bare breasts and left her naked in the back. She tied the sides of the top together at the base of her spine.

A long black jersey skirt with a split high up the side hugged her body and the red-beaded braids added drama. She could see where the soft mound of her pelvis extended ever so slightly forward of her hips, and wondered if others would notice. Turning to look at her backside in the full-length mirror, she was pleased by what she saw. And why not? Hadn't she done enough squats, not to mention all those hours spent jogging? Her firm, taut buttocks looked rounder than usual under the skirt's sleek, black mantle.

As she walked toward the door in her platform sandals, she

watched the way the fabric glided over her buttocks, subtly showcasing the crack between her cheeks.

Leaving her room at seven o'clock to meet Ross at the boat triggered memories of other erotic encounters. The most powerful ones were the first. They started in her early teens, when her father wouldn't let her date. Incensed by his limits, she had let her desires branch out in a variety of ways. Titillated by the forbidden, she sought out fertile ground for experimentation. Perhaps that's why she chose Tony. While he lived only eight miles away, it might as well have been 10,000. Clean cut enough, he pumped his testosterone through the chrome pipes of souped up cars—lots of them, in fact. Like other kids in that odd town, his business was knowing all about those fast, daring machines. Customized, sleek, and a bit wicked, Tony's cars were hot. That's why, Lexi guessed, she went with him.

Her body was lithe and supple. Like today, friends responded to what they called her love of life. She hoped for the courage to once again steer herself through life with innocent desire and not second-guess herself. That's what she wanted tonight: delicious spontaneity. The type she had before she'd become a woman who worried about consequences—emotional or otherwise.

Once on the boat, she enjoyed the anonymity and the friendly way she was jostled by the crowd. When the pace picked up, she headed for the bow and breathed the sea air down into her chest to quell some jitters. She was aware of the first moment Ross spotted her far forward in the boat, and from that point on she was the object of his attention. All she had to do was swish her plaited hair from one side to the other to feel his head turn. When she resisted the urge to glance his way, he'd issue a cough and a loud command to one of his crew, causing her to turn, following her body's impulse, and steady her eyes on his face. Lexi looked out to sea and took in an extra deep breath. This dance between them signaled a perfect premeditated tryst, and Lexi was full of playful thoughts and ways to keep his interest going as they stood far away from each other in a crowd.

In time he came for Lexi and asked her to dance. After a couple of turns, they ducked out. Ross in the lead, head down, moving rapidly as the band beat out a Caribbean favorite. Lexi felt protected by his graceful stride that moved her forward. She felt everything and nothing at the same time. Anchored by the even pressure of his hand as he led the way to his car, her enthusiasm kept pace with the speeded up clicking of the red beads on her plaited hair.

Behind the wheel, Ross seemed propelled by the animal instinct that routes mating partners to a safe place. They sped around the island's curves to his remote home, his eyes frequently glancing at Lexi, even as he navigated a treacherous stretch of the road.

Lexi, knowing little about Ross, was eager to explore his habitat. The colonial house might offer clues about her soon-to-be lover. She was charmed by the rich contrast of the dark wood against the light walls. There was a modern beveled-glass coffee table, but the high ceilings, tall shutters, and ceiling fans were markings of a different world.

The furnishings bespoke Ross's affluence and were features that gave her other information. More space than usual between the pieces gave the room an uncluttered look. Unusual items—an antique rocker and an oversized vase—added a hint of mystery. But what struck Lexi most was the serenity, unlike the home she shared with Jake.

Ross's attention seemed fragmented until they were in his bedroom. Lexi sensed this was his safe spot, and felt his mind and his body slow down. She was the one who now felt a sense of urgency.

The peace vanished when he grabbed her shoulders tightly and kissed her hard. Too impatient to untie or unhitch her halter top, he forced it upwards as his palms squeezed and rippled her flesh. Lexi liked the way he took control of her so fast, pressing his firm hands on her back, then using them to mound her breasts. A thumb hardened her nipple. His mouth, like a sea lamprey, sucked and pulled at her lips.

To feel unconscious so soon was uncanny. When had they undressed? Completely under his spell, Lexi moved ahead from the inside out. He pulled her to the bed. They didn't make eye contact until he was far enough away to give her some perspective. As he caressed her fleshy pubis and moved like a salamander across the sheets, his face came into view. She watched with wet anticipation as he lowered himself into the wide spread opening to her soul, then she smiled from afar, silently stroking him with her eyes.

Lexi was open to the entire spectrum of their lovemaking. She felt secure as her eyes slowly panned the beautiful room, then her spirit rested in the glow. The dark, rich, four-poster bed was covered by a fresh blue and peach striped spread. Pulled back so artfully yet effortlessly into soft folds, the bed covering was a delicate backdrop to their firm, tan bodies. She felt suspended in a Shangri-La of the senses.

Lexi lay back and watched Ross tenderly lick her pulsing flesh. She enjoyed his style—skilled, focused, and fully absorbed. Her tissues swelled in response to his touch. Starting from a subterranean core, her tender clitoris grew harder and harder. She started to twist her body, then steadied it. Losing her focus, she tensed up.

He could be quick. He could get rough. Or he could love

her, at least for the night. She yearned to feel that sweet appreciation that trickles through a man when a woman gives herself over to him. She understood the way a fellow could care about you when you satisfy his needs. But certainly a lot of pretty faces came to him in that way. The thought of all those others made her uncomfortable. As she reached out to stop him, he must have sensed the tension within her. Ross whispered her name, murmuring the things she needed to hear: that he was there for her completely tonight, and that he ached for her.

Lexi trusted Ross instinctively and breathed in deeply as she stilled her body. She would show him every wild and sensuous part of her and would let him do as he wished. Happier now to know she could give her most vulnerable, loving essence to him, she lost herself in the pleasure of discovery.

It was a moment of the deepest intimacy and trust. Intense stimulation of her uncovered clit drove her to her limit. She expected she'd close down, shift her body, and they'd move ahead to his genitals. That's the way it went with Jake. Step one. Step two. Step, who really cares. She'd know that time was running out, that it was her turn to do him, then onto penetration, and what he wanted most—a good night's sleep.

This was different, and her soul knew it. She shivered as Ross looked deep into her treasure—her core. As he pressed back her labia for a fuller view and moved his tongue near her once-buried pearl, she spread her legs wider. Alternately licking and sucking, with the gentleness extended to a newborn baby, he played with her clit. Lexi's moans grew to giggles while her body lay nearly still and she dared to share herself fully. She began to rock. Her whimpers both softened and lengthened, building toward frenzy, ecstasy. Then Lexi thrust her clitoris further and further forward into his velvet tongue, giving him everything she had.

She was electric with pleasure. Basking in the warmth, she took more of what he had to give. Her pelvis rolled, then rocked. Her spasms started as her voice, a mix of far ranging notes from the musical scale, rang free. Gasping for air, she reeled as Ross locked her hips with his hands. Breaking free, her pelvis catapulted them both into the chaos that spread so naturally from his lips to her lower body. Then Lexi twisted to the side when she could no longer separate her wild gyrations from her screams.

Coaxing her back to consciousness, Ross asked, "Where did you come from, my goddess?"

"From my memories and dreams," Lexi whispered hoarsely, trying to calm herself enough to speak. Through a smile just starting to break, she continued, "And I have more of them. I'll show you." Then she reached for his shoulder and moved down the sheets with grace. Thank God for all those Monday evening yoga classes.

Their heads were at about the same height for just a moment before they changed positions. Ross turned over on his back, as Lexi moved between his legs. As she went, she tousled Ross's hair and looked down at the beauty and strength of his sphinx-like frame. The soft liquid glow of her eyes matched his, and they locked together in a stare that spoke of the mystery she wanted to unravel.

Lexi moved naturally, re-enacting a ritual, ancient as a temple dance immortalized on papyrus. Nestling herself between his legs, she cupped his penis in her palm and smiled as she stroked his hardened flesh. Through the amber light in the room, she could see sprigs of the coarse, dark hair that decorated his chest, burnished by the loving Barbados sun.

Propped up with his arms crossed behind his head, Ross's misty smile made her aware that it was his turn to feel shy, maybe scared, as she had moments before. Sliding her hand up and down his shaft, she let the pressure build until his eyes drifted shut, and she could feel a thin patina of nectar on his testicles.

Lexi took Ross into her mouth with relish. He was dark as chocolate, probably from the nude sunbathing for which Barbados seemed created. It was like closing her eyes and putting a brick of Godiva on her tongue. Slowly, she lowered him into the moist, dark interior of her mouth. Playfully, she swirled her tongue around him. No longer able to separate the fuzz of her tongue from his rich chocolate coating with its intense flavor, she paused to take in air, then took him in her mouth again. Ecstasy encircled them. Then the chocolate hit the roof of her mouth. Lips closed, she stroked his pulsing cock. They were one.

Lexi glanced up at Ross and saw that the expression on his face had changed. No longer the man in charge, his relaxed face was as uncomplicated as that of a babe at rest. His tanned body had an amber glow. Lying before her, he seemed suspended in the space between his imagination and her touch.

Opening his eyes, he pulled her toward him. His energy pierced her like darts. "And now, m' lady, I have something very special for you."

Lexi's eyes flashed when he slapped her briskly on the buttocks and turned her on her back. Arched above her, he dropped down to devour her breasts, like a hungry seagull wresting a clam from the beach as a snack. Enthralled, Lexi stared him in the eye and saw the fire. Sensing he'd return the ecstasy she'd brought him, her body was in flames. Threatening to grip him ever tighter with her fingernails, she made desire clear. That's when he thrust himself inside her and without mercy tried to tear them both apart.

Lexi lurched, then gasped, then threw herself into the bon-
fire he'd started. Alive, euphoric, and overwhelmed. Would he
ever stop? Feeling him drag her vagina in one direction, then
the other, she was in sexual agony.

Her screams spiked his desire. Grabbing her shoulder, he
quickly turned her around. She was greedy with anticipation
and ready for anything. Surprised to feel him glide once more
into her snug vagina, she rolled like the whitecaps she'd seen
that afternoon. Lexi felt as though she were at sea again. For a
moment, she imagined her body as the ocean. Ross was a majestic ship, moving over, through, and inside her all at once. His
mass was in harmony with her purpose. He was neither too
heavy nor too rough for her. His needs defined her capabilities,
just as her nature bred his opportunity. Gulping for more air
between the shouts, she could no longer distinguish his sounds
from hers.

"Give it to me. Give me all you've got," he commanded.

Abandon turned into chaos. Like an angry sea, the boat
rocked until it nearly splintered apart. The waves lashed the
side of the ship and the decks cleared as never before.
Commotion gave way to beauty. The captain made peace with
the sea goddess. And Venus had her way at last. The black
clouds receded and a new day was born.

Lexi felt a charge run through her body, then his. She shook
as she followed the feeling. He seemed to have an urge to
plunge to her depths, those beyond her body that were buried
in her soul. Did he want to release everything inside him into
her—even his disappointments? His ferocity made her feel as if
he wanted to solder himself permanently to her life-giving
forces. It was as though he'd crashed into a wild and raging sea
at its most fetching moment, with iridescent sparks rising from
the dancing waves. She yearned for a moment that would last
forever. She surrendered.

Once again deep inside, Ross bathed her innards. A whirl of images grew like an instant tropical garden. Her clitoris and labia pulsed uncontrollably, as if to greet and guide him home. Fresh from her deep-sea dive, she could still taste all the colors and shapes of his exquisite flesh.

Ross withdrew from her with momentum. Something was changing, catching Lexi up in yet another fevered pitch. Ross stood up, heading for the bathroom. His cock was still perpendicular from his loins. Lexi could feel his confusion.

Her mind whirred like the mirror glass ball she remembered from her first prom. As reflections of their lovemaking twirled through her soul, each sliver of the tryst spun her round and round with centrifugal force and time stood still. She felt she sparkled, like the mirrored ball.

When he returned to her, it was awhile before they spoke. Nuzzling the top of Lexi's head, Ross squeezed her body closer, running his palms up and down her smooth back. Bumping against the red balls at the end of each plaited braid, he laughed and prodded, "Tell me about your dreams."

"I just did," she said.

"Your sounds were definitely better than any story I ever heard in school," he teased.

"I'm very happy," she said, as she returned his squeeze, wanting to savor, not dissect, the experience.

Lexi awakened first at about five o'clock. The light coming through the dark wood shutters cast a new reality on the encounter. Bringing her knees tight against her chest as she turned sideways on the bed, she let thoughts of the day wash away many of the midnight sensations. Hugging herself in this fetal position, she gathered together her happiness and her ambivalence. Feeling lighter, Lexi lay back in the pretty yet mysterious room, stretching out on her bed of dreams for the last time.

Ross awoke with a start, and with desire. To love her again could make their parting difficult. It would be hard to get through the day with her under his skin.

He glanced over at Lexi, eyes wide open and looking at the ceiling. He bet that people always remembered her face and knew he would. "And still so beautiful," he whispered as he pulled her toward him.

Lexi giggled when his hand moved so urgently between her legs. Still taken by the mystery of the encounter, she was eager to explore the rich sensations he renewed for her. He stirred her clitoris and it hardened quickly.

"And you have such a lot of work to do today," she said, smiling as she smoothed his chest with her hands.

Turning onto her knees, she lifted herself up and straddled Ross's muscular frame.

Stroking his cock like a leathery horn, Lexi squeezed and teased him. Then she scrambled forward on the sheets, while her hard nipples brushed over his curly chest hairs. Bearing down on her palms, she was as steady as a pony at the starting gate.

Eager to feel him inside her again, she mounted Ross briskly. Spiked by the angle of the fit, Lexi quivered. Making small circles with her hips, she basked in the palpitations. Hot geysers bubbled within her, and she envisioned riding at breakneck speed on the wide-open, Western plains. That's when she saw the hot springs burst, leaping like fire.

Straightening up, she heaved forward then back like a child's favorite rocking horse. As the momentum built, Ross reached up to hold her hands. Happy to turn over the reins, she joined up with him. Bringing Ross toward the front of her pelvis, she gripped tightly. Clenching his cock as she drew in her vaginal walls, Lexi felt playful. Back and forth they rolled, his penis now her trusty companion, her lovable friend.

As Ross loosened his hands, Lexi arched back and yelped. Moaning as his fingers tickled her clitoris, she relished the bliss. Pelvis swollen, she broke loose. Lexi shook with abandon and cried out in glee. She slowed when he levered her up with his own hot spring. Nearly airborne, she rested high on the foamy sensations. Quiescent again, she fell back in the saddle of his lap as soon as she saw his face writhe with delicious pain.

Lexi dozed with her head on Ross's chest and her leg threaded between his thighs. She awoke with a start as the room filled with light. She needed to get back to the hotel, her room, and the beach to get a hold of herself. Things were happening so quickly. Her whole world was in flux, and she needed to put it in perspective. The joy, the celebration. The mystery. The sheer beauty of it all. Abundance. Exhilaration.

And she needed to return soon, before the other guests started to stir. If she were seen coming back in her evening gear, her long, black skirt and red silk halter top, it would be harder to duck the lecherous invitations she'd been getting from the older American men. All the small talk about her husband back home started to haunt her as she calculated how quickly she'd lose that good-girl image.

"Ross," Lexi said, as she touched his shoulder and looked eagerly into his eyes. "I feel so wonderful, but I really have to get back." She needed to be alone to understand the seismic shifts within her. Unexpected fissures were fleshing out a new terrain, and probably new paths to explore within.

With a strained smile on his face, Ross brushed his hand along the side of her head, leaned down to kiss her on the lips, and said, "Aye, mate."

The ride to the hotel had a different flavor from the night before. Ross stopped, as planned, at the mouth of the entrance to the resort. A quick hug and kiss, ones that just as easily could have passed between friends, served to disengage them. "I'll call you later, love," he said. "How about a drive this afternoon?"

"Sounds great," she said, as her heart warmed at the prospect. "Between now and then, I'll figure out what to do with all this electricity," Lexi teased, rubbing her arms with her palms.

He looked intently at her face. "You know, you scare me a bit, love," he said.

"Mmm," Lexi responded. "I know just what you mean."

Swinging her hips freely as she passed the red hibiscus bushes along the road into Sandy Lane, Lexi was alive with pleasure. Back at her sun drenched nest she'd be able to replay the first taste of her dream. Maybe she simply manifested the whole encounter during that life-changing swim. But right now, Lexi was in touch with feelings she'd nearly forgotten. Last night she'd unleashed sensations that put her soul on alert. She was still tingling, and wondered what would happen next.

No matter. Last night was real. The dream about a life filled with sensual pleasure was grounded and she had the day to relive the night.

The first person Lexi saw on the way to her room was Steven, the handsome waiter who'd greeted her with such a beatific smile yesterday afternoon. His eyes sparkled this morning as well, although their exchange was quicker than usual. They acknowledged each other in a friendly way, then went about their business.

When Lexi looked at Steven, she remembered how the sheer beauty of the people and the island had piqued her desire. For years, Lexi had thought about making changes in her life. But those hefty battles within her mind dissolved in Barbados. Lexi had opened up a new world just by trusting herself. Wrapped up in all the sensations, she felt centered and as complete as a sea horse, bobbing solo in the foamy surf. All she knew for sure was that she was happy in a new way. Her heart was open to the surges of love and tenderness that flowed like gentle waves over sun-kissed sand.

Lexi's body relaxed as she came to her room. There lay some solitude; she would stretch out and enjoy the euphoria. But as Lexi opened the door, her mood changed. At first, her room seemed dark and somewhat ordinary. The hotel palate of soft green fabrics and mid-tone woods was soulless compared to the room she'd shared with Ross, with its delicate floral patterns and majestic, dark wood furniture. Would everything else in her life seem so much less than what she'd remembered?

A bath, then breakfast, followed by the beach—that ought to work. By noon she'd know what to do about the fear of losing her newfound self so soon. As she drew her bath, she had a chance to look closely at herself in the mirror and saw something better than what she remembered. Her doeskin, heart-shaped face set off her green eyes, which were brighter than usual today. The sun had bleached her brows and the iridescent blondish brown hairs gave a lift to her face. The nose she'd always disliked now seemed dignified—one that might belong to an Egyptian queen or a Pharaoh's wife. Her mouth was relaxed. Even she could see that her bow-shaped lips, without lipstick, appeared tender and kind.

She liked what she saw—a good woman. Pretty, yes, and on this occasion her energies lit up the space surrounding her. She looked like someone she could trust. And why not? She used her instincts to make good choices, and life was getting better.

Lexi lowered herself into the tub and took on the hardest thoughts first. Jake, her shadow husband. Ironically, she felt particularly close to him—his vulnerabilities and his hopes. The notion of separating herself from Jake took on the proportions of a natural disaster. A divorce could lash her to bits, striking with the force of a hurricane. Her neck and shoulders felt tight as she leaned forward to turn off the water. Sitting back, Lexi stilled herself. Not sure how she could give him enough support, Lexi had a hunch that maybe he'd do better without her.

The image of a divorce was dark and overpowering. Conjuring up the images of a pale pink lotus, Lexi focused on its roots and how Shakti had said they served as an anchor during monsoons. She could feel those same roots feeding her now.

Then Lexi pictured herself as an innocent child. Spirited, curious, often carefree. Another rush of feelings from college years took hold. Hadn't she marshaled enough discipline then, and, later, at work, so that her life would have focus? How regularly she'd sacrificed ordinary pleasures, molding herself into a strong woman, able to chart her own destiny. But she knew in her gut that discipline alone did not make a marriage.

The steely image of divorce cut through her again like a machete. Lexi wasn't too timid to solve problems. After all, hadn't some of the worst projects at Bradford Communications eventually turned out pretty well? Slugging it out with colleagues, hadn't she usually found a better way?

At work she treated conflict as the route to new solutions, a tool that drove her success. But at home, Jake made her feel small. She could no longer share her enthusiasm for her job without inviting sarcasm. Jake hated her work about as much as he despised his own. After the daily battle with academic fiefdoms, he beat a retreat to his study. Was it just a matter of time before his whole life would become a series of disappointments?

What about failure? Could she accept that she hadn't been able to do what others do with great satisfaction? Could she dodge imaginary barbs about being a quitter? It was hard to know whether divorce was a tough choice or the right choice.

Lexi wanted her life to expand in meaningful ways. At home,

she felt as though she was contracting. As Jake retreated from his colleagues and his frustrations, he pulled her down in ways that seemed to be multiplying. Separated from him now, she could still feel his manipulation and fear.

Right now she and Jake were like two paths diverging in the woods. All she wanted was to take the one that was hers. Relief washed over her like healing sea spray. With it came the image of someone who, like her, was reaching out to the world. Someone who liked a challenge. This man she envisioned had a lotus heart and a healing touch. Coiled inside him was a vision of a better world.

Perhaps he'd admire her guts, even stoke her courage, then help mop the blood from her emotional wounds when she failed. Yes, she still believed that her purpose was to build loving relationships. How easy it might be to live a committed life with someone on the same wave length.

Lexi dreamed up more erotic interludes. Ones that tapped her deep, sensual reserves. Perhaps she'd find a lover who would walk with her along the ocean edge, then tumble into the brush, and surrender under the stars. She'd look for someone gentle, confident, and open to all that life offered. She had those qualities and they longed for a match. The image of such a delicious union conjured up sensations from the night before and she gathered her knees to her chest, rocking back and forth in the warm water. Yet, even as she imagined she was in Ross's arms again, feeling his rough, sea-worn hands searching out the silky respite between her legs, Lexi knew he was not the lotus heart for whom she searched. Soon enough, their sexual storm would pass, and there would be little else to hold them together.

Emerging from the water, she wrapped herself in an oversized bath towel, then rubbed hard to polish her skin and slough off yesterday's dead cells.

Out on her porch, nestled in her chaise longue, she wrote a note to him that emerged from the softest place in her heart.

Dear Ross,

Last night I was as happy as I can remember being in the arms of a lover.

As I think back to the moment when I first saw you, Ross, I probably sensed the possibility. Your eyes spoke of worlds I wanted to explore. From your stance, I could feel your confidence and courage. And your banter with your mates revealed a natural, caring command.

From the few words we shared, I understood something about your sensuality. Easy, yet deep. A hint of reverence, and the hope— or was it an expectation?—that pleasure would be mutual.

But about last night. Buddhists would call it bliss. Kids would say it was awesome. I think it was love. The kind of love that builds quickly between two levelheaded but savvy people with deep underground reservoirs of feeling. Ones, that haven't been properly tapped in much too long a time.

How does that work? When enough water from a deep, subterranean river is caught under thick layers of rock, something eventually happens. Desperate, the trapped water searches for a way out. The hunt for a new path creates so much pressure that the water breaks through the earth's surface.

For me, and perhaps for you, that's a river of feeling, trapped for all too long by the mind, by the "shoulds". We broke free last night. Naturally. Powerfully. Completely. May our lives become more like our respective artesian springs.

I'm wandering from my purpose now. I know our hours together will change my life— irreversibly and for the better. Our time was short. I had hoped to touch and kiss you, feel you inside me, and

*once again transcend an all-too-often ordinary time and space
which until now I'd known simply as my life. But intuition tells me
this is where we should end.*

With love,
Lexi

She sealed the letter, brushed it wistfully with her lips, and
left it for Ross at the front desk. Had they met again, the words
would be different. The risk was that their talk would be tepid
or trite. What they'd shared was too precious for that; better to
give back in some small way a sliver of the beauty he'd given
her.

Lexi called the airlines, and lucked into a cancellation on the
next flight out. She was going home to a new life.

SPRING

I am certain of nothing but the holiness of the Heart's
affections and the truth of the Imagination—
What the imagination seizes as Beauty must be truth—
whether it existed before or not.

~ JOHN KEATS

L exi smiled as she snaked down the dark stairwell of her
favorite Italian restaurant, Armando's. Lunches with
Shakti always perked her up. She felt younger than her
thirty-two years. Armando's was where they always had their
best discussions—those which triggered a different way of
knowing. Sometimes their talks prompted insights. Often she
and Shakti made plans. But mostly they stuck to the core business of pumping good energy along the pathways to and from
the heart—all to improve each other's lives.

Boston's North End warmed and reassured her. It was the
safety that came from years of Mafia bosses routing out anyone
who didn't cooperate. Theirs was the business of eliminating
threats, regardless of whether they came from friends or family.
The North End had rules to uphold, even now. It was a swatch

of Boston where people watched out for one another. Those infrequent times when impulse and passion broke loose, the residents knew what to do. The patchwork of apartments and neighborhood shops were the first line of defense, but the real healing took place in the restaurants. No one knew if it started with the pasta, the red sauce, or the Chianti.

That was what she needed—that and Shakti. Lexi's promotion three months ago shot through her life like an errant arrow. After eight years at Bradford Communications she was a vice president who wielded considerable power and had a travel budget anybody would love. So why did every day seem like a hollow, eerie echo of the one before?

She needed something besides ambition on which to travel through life. She never regretted divorcing Jake. While she was still searching for someone with a lotus heart, her life had substance. Daily she immersed herself in her work, coming up with one idea after another. Creativity sustained her and, like poetry, was a conduit to her emotions. And there was always adventure.

The deals. Lots of them simmering, brewing, or waiting to be reeled in. She had a second sense about which ones were going somewhere, and that helped her stay focused and conserve energy. Bradford Communications had deep pockets, and a universal reach. She enjoyed the week in London last month, with all those television executives finalizing plans for a new miniseries. Still, some piece of her self was missing. Shakti could help her sort out these conflicting needs and make sense of it all.

As her Ferragamos hit the worn tread of the last step, she entered the restaurant and scanned for her college friend. Tall and imposing, Shakti, just steps ahead, had stopped at a table for four and placed her large shopping bag on one of the chairs. Smiling at the maitre d', she'd successfully commandeered extra space for the precious words she and Lexi would share. Lexi feasted on the familiar warmth of Shakti's eyes, and wished hers lit up as easily. The contrast with her dark, rich Indian skin was a sensation. Lexi had always enjoyed watching Shakti dazzle a man.

Lexi let out a deep sigh, relieved to know she wouldn't have to wait for Shakti to break from a lengthy team meeting. As usual, Lexi had brought *The Times* and could always mull over her to-do lists. Ever since Adler, LaSalle and Thomas saddled Shakti with the task of training young architects, their lunches had gotten shorter. But today she was on time.

Giving her friend a big hug, Lexi said, "I don't know what I'd do without these escapes. It's great to be out of the war zone."

"Another acquisition?"

"Could be. Except for a zillion obstacles. Hockhauser has a knack for them."

Al Hockhauser, CEO of Bradford Communications, was Lexi's new boss. They had both been at Bradford for the past eight years, but now she reported directly to him. An aggressive, authoritarian executive, he was well-known for getting the last dollar out of a deal.

"Another siege of terror?"

"I haven't had a good night's sleep in weeks."

"This has to stop."

"So, you're part of the group that thinks life gets better?"

"It does if you have the kind of work that gives you more control over your time."

Lexi threw her head back and laughed. "Right. Like architects who muse for weeks on end, then work twenty hours a day to meet deadlines."

"We do have the musing."

"True. I'd be glad to muse about anything," she said, exhausted and discouraged.

"How's your love life?" Shakti asked.

"About the same. Nothing to report," Lexi said.

"Why do you think that is?" Shakti asked tenderly.

Lexi grabbed for a hard roll, broke it open, and swept giant flecks of crust away with the side of her hand. "Bad karma."

Laughing, Shakti countered, "Won't work with me. All you need to do is turn the wheels of karma. Motion becomes ecstasy."

"Turn? Is that a new book? Haven't noticed it in the stores."

"Look harder. It's all in the *Kama Sutra*."

"Haven't we done this before?"

"Not this part, apparently. The turning. The dance."

"Yeah."

"You know, it's the central piece of a vast body of knowledge. The science of love."

"Must be something else I took pass-fail."

"The big thing is the framework. Sexual passion follows the same laws of motion as an object rolling down a hill. It's natural. Passion increases by degrees."

"Damn. I knew I had some missing parts, but no idea how many."

"Lexi. I don't mean to be intrusive. Or bossy. But you know this," Shakti said, seeming agitated and afraid of making matters worse. "All you need to do is remember it. And none of it works when you're exhausted."

"Do I get to go back and practice the clasp of the serpent? Or maybe the union of milk and water would be more appropriate."

With her lips forming a kiss, Shakti said, "Start with the big picture. Imagination. Commitment. Practice."

"I'm beginning to think I should have been born into an Indian family. I'd know more. Anyway, let's order. Imagination can wait."

While their conversation was lively, Lexi felt numb, only half connected, puzzling through the complicated emotions that swirled within.

Shakti understood and was trying to help. But Lexi feared what she wanted might be out of reach. Maybe Shakti was right. If she slowed down a bit, her inner life might surface more often and fill the void. She needed to make a big change, not just take a new approach to building a relationship. Solitude would be more productive than dating anyone—and it would give her inner life more room to grow.

Lunch ended much too soon. They wrapped up the other details of their lives and made plans to stay in touch. Walking back to her office, Lexi enjoyed the changing seasons. Spring was her favorite. The light seemed especially bright after winter's darkness. She remembered playing hopscotch on puddle luscious streets and the memory lifted her spirits. A New Englander at heart, she was wedded to rituals that marked each season. From Groundhog Day to Easter, she watched the earth soften and bloom. By May Day, her home was always a kaleidoscope of color—all the way to her birthday in June.

Back in her office, she couldn't shake off the hurt feelings Shakti's sharp observations had caused. Hundreds of times, Lexi and Shakti had discussed Shakti's belief that a life was nothing more than the soul's attempt to realize its highest aspirations. Shakti must think she was stuck, or in trouble. She seemed to suggest that Lexi was resisting or ignoring a deeper part of herself, and that she should spend time alone to let those images from the soul break through and move her forward.

Lexi was in awe of Shakti's ease in discussing sensitive subjects, and appreciated the way she gently steered her toward a new perception. Fortunately, they hadn't gotten bogged down by the nuances of passion, and how they viewed it differently.

Lexi felt that passion fueled her, and that when she lived from its vital source of energy, she made good choices. It was as simple as that. It was like a natural well. Shakti's view was a bit heady. She believed that passion was the best way to direct the soul's search for truth, but wasn't an end itself. A person defined dharma or purpose first, then applied passion to the quest. Today, that difference in their views struck Lexi as more critical than in the past. It was not that Lexi felt she had missed the point before, just that her emphasis had been different. Still, it was a bit confusing.

Anyway, the psychic pain was new. Lexi knew that it was time to take action to end the loneliness. If she understood Shakti correctly, she was to spend time alone, use her imagination. That way she could get in touch with images from her soul. That's when her life would change.

What did this have to do with men right now? Maybe she'd been focusing on the wrong kind of man. Startled by the phone's ring, Lexi picked up her direct line to Rose.

"Yes, Rose."

"It's Shakti."

"Okay. I'll pick up," she said in a raspy tone. Then shifting in her chair, she cleared her voice. "Well hello, my dear. More proof that you're my salvation. I was just going over the edge."

"Live on the edge. Don't go over. You're still Ravi's godmother, you know."

"His own Auntie Mame. Your son will always be safe with me."

"What are you up to?"

"God knows."

"I'm sorry if I hurt your feelings at lunch," Shakti said quietly.

"You know, when I feel pain," Lexi said slowly, as if understanding something for the first time, "you help me be more conscious of what's really going on with me. Which is just a long way of saying thanks. I'll keep you posted."

"I'm here," Shakti said quietly.

⌒

Each morning when Lexi left Brookline for work, she breathed the morning air deep into her belly and down to her toes. Today the dawn light washed her body. The effects of spring were everywhere. The pearly morning sky even softened the polished black branches of the naked trees in her yard. With each sign of spring, she could be sure the stiff, hard landscape around her red brick Georgian home would change.

Driving to work, Lexi noticed more differences. People were walking faster, their heads held higher and faces relaxed. Some people smiled. Something was happening to the neurotransmitters in the brain. She felt the kind of energy that signaled a new beginning. But soon, once Brookline was behind her, Lexi mostly felt tired.

When she walked into her office, she noticed a beautiful pot of salmon tulips on her desk. Her secretary, Rose, followed her in. In her brusque yet motherly way explained, "I thought we needed something new around here. Got some azaleas for me. I'll take care of them both."

"Rose, you're the best," Lexi said, and gave her a quick hug. "I was just thinking about this gorgeous spring, and this clinches it."

Before she'd finished hanging up her coat, Rose buzzed her on the intercom. "Mr. Hockhauser's on line one."

"Lexi, the satellite programming deal looks better than I first thought. Just had breakfast with Jones. Says we'd have solid partners."

"You mean the Starlight Group?" Lexi said, recalling the prospectus Al had sent her.

"They're as good as they come."

"So I've heard."

"The big play will be the Asian market. It's the twist that might make the numbers work. We know as much as there is to know about the economics in the U.S. and Europe."

"Asia's tricky. Lots of people. Very little discretionary income."

"The focus is on big cities. Apartment buildings, you know."

"Yeah."

"Hong Kong. Tokyo. Seoul. That's where most of the money is."

"What about the competition?"

"That's what I want you to figure out. Can you go over there? Meet with some of their people?"

She took a moment before she said, "Yeah, I guess so." Then her eyes lit up at the prospect. "What's the timing?"

"A.S.A.P."

"Maybe I could get ready by Sunday, if I get some help with the visas," she said, conjuring up more than a business deal as she spoke.

"Say. Thanks a million. Have Rose call Jones about the visas."

Putting down the phone, Lexi shook her head in disbelief. All this, just when the job was feeling stale.

Five days later, as her plane made its final approach into Hong Kong, Lexi's enthusiasm knew no bounds. Flipping back and forth through five guidebooks during the flight, she knew that seeing just a smidgen of the city's most famous sites would be enough to dissolve the haze that had settled over her life. That's really why she wanted to make the trip. Lexi hoped to run her fingers through yards of embroidered silk. Smell and savor spicy, smoky teas, and eat Peking duck. Meanwhile, she'd put together a solid plan for dealing with the business issues; she knew what information she needed and with whom she'd need to meet. The rest of the trip would be time alone, a chance to commune with her soul in one of the most exotic cities in the world.

As Lexi deplaned, she noticed a well-dressed man with a white sign. It read, "Miss Lankford." Whatever happened to the Ms. battle? Who cared? She'd long since decided to define her personal world according to her own boundaries, and she liked to see how far they could stretch.

After an easy check-in at the Peninsula, she had time for a quick walk before dinner. Her travel agent had insisted she stay at the Peninsula, and now she understood why. It put her in Kowloon, on the edge of the mainland, across the harbor from Hong Kong Island. From the tenth floor of the Peninsula, Hong Kong looked like a diamond. At night, the Rock, as it was called, was painted in lights, mostly white with a neon fringe around the water where the biggest global companies trumpeted their names. Products. Services. If it existed, you could find it in Hong Kong. Lexi thought of the city as an invitation. Like an oversized piece of jewelry, studded with a mix of tiny white and yellow diamonds that shimmered in all directions, it asked to be enjoyed. An oval trinket with scaly, pavé skin.

Her love affair with Hong Kong started on the boat. Eager to see some of the sights before her ten o'clock meeting, she awoke early and boarded the ferry from Kowloon to Hong Kong. Lexi loved the mix of people, and was caught up in the rush as bodies pressed together on the gangway. After the echoes from so many feet hitting the floorboards subsided, she enjoyed the quiet and could feel her inner world unfolding.

Where had she ever seen so many people packed together, so early in the morning? Despite the crowd, they relaxed easily in the grip of the world's most densely populated city. Some dressed in high fashion clothes and read English language newspapers. Others wore jeans and T-shirts, and were ready to work in one of the countless shops or restaurants. Older kids clustered together in their immaculate blue uniforms, while younger ones were watched over by their amahs. There was comfort in the subtle connection between such varied lives. Lexi was part of the group that mostly gazed out over Victoria Harbor.

By week's end she felt like a native. Pushing her way on board with Tai Chi like moves, she'd fashioned a spot toward the bow. Back far enough to avoid the spray, she enjoyed being one of the first to leave the boat and climb onto the island. It was such an exotic world that she had trouble believing it had once been a British colony. By Friday, she'd heard plenty of stories from folks in the Starlight Group. All week, they'd educated and entertained her. She particularly liked learning how the British had resisted China's ban on opium in the early 1800s. To protect its business interests, Britain waged war to win a treaty or a piece of land where they could live under their own flag. That was when China gave Britain Hong Kong. Considered a barren island with hardly a house on it, it became one of the greatest ports in the world.

Her work week had been productive. Lexi had won the trust of her prospective colleagues, and they had promised to have the information she needed by next week. The weekend was hers. Heading to a dinner party, she felt the adventure begin when she left the hotel and realized she was one of the most exotic creatures on the street. With soft blond curls cascading just below her chin, she was the one who stood out in Hong Kong amid head after head of thick, straight locks—the type and texture she'd always coveted. But tonight, her hair was exactly the way she wanted it, and she wouldn't have changed a frizzed end.

Lexi had her first glimpse of how the wealthy lived when

Wong, the driver Mary and Ted had sent for her, wheeled his Mercedes into the circular entrance of a stunning white building near the top of the Rock. Sleeker than those around it, the handsome building looked new. Lexi wished Shakti could see the wide glass windows and the turquoise-tinted aluminum trim. She knew she'd appreciate the lush landscaping, too.

Lexi squealed when Mary, her mother's friend, opened the door. She looked wonderful, so petite and elegant. After a warm greeting, Mary took Lexi by the arm, as if for extra support, and ushered her into the living room to meet the other guests.

Lexi loved the collection of vases on the table just inside the room. The deep red tones of the carved cinnabar were stunning against the cobalt blue on the Chinese porcelain. She'd heard from her mother about Mary's passion for art and her fabulous collection. Lexi's eyes darted from one end of the room to the other. Japanese woodblock prints. Carved Indian statues. A dark green, bronze Cambodian rain drum that was used as a table. All mixed up with the playful colors of Picasso, Miro, and Matisse lithographs. The room danced, just as Hong Kong gyrated outside its eight-foot wraparound windows, and Lexi felt encased in Asian splendor.

The impact of the decor receded as she studied a man standing by a built-in bar. When Mary's husband, Ted, turned to make introductions, Lexi felt an odd pull toward this guest. Her eyes had picked him out when she did her initial scan of the room. Her gaze lingered on his frame. She guessed him to be about five feet, nine inches—about her height. Probably in his mid-thirties. Overall she thought of him as dark, or maybe mysterious. Perhaps the mystique had to do with how he held his angular body. When she touched the cushion of his hand, she felt an unusual warmth. A smile spread gently across his face and his eyes brightened.

When the conversation between the four of them began, she pulled back. The man they called Zheng Wu had a way of taking charge of the subject being discussed. Lexi wondered if he was the type of man who always had to be in command. Could he ever give up enough control to be intimate? Playful? Maybe he'd feel too vulnerable. Lexi toyed with fantasies about the other people she'd meet tonight.

Much as she enjoyed the other guests, particularly the newspaper columnist and the banker, her curiosity centered again on Zheng Wu. Raised in Hong Kong and educated at Stanford, he had an appealing sophistication. Lexi made guesses about the wealth of this heir to a shipping fortune and whether it made him less sensitive to others. Did he lead a life of excess? Suffer pangs of social conscience?

She found his wit disarming and liked the ease with which he told stories. The one about a character in a Run Run Shaw movie seemed particularly revealing. With zeal, he described an agile crook in the film whose greed was his undoing. Obsessed, he thought of nothing but his money. The trait pierced his core and eventually gave him away when the police linked his handwriting to the crime. Instead of using only five lines to create the Chinese word for money, he added an extra stroke.

Intoxicated by Zheng's style, Lexi watched closely as he talked. She liked to watch how he used his body to emphasize his ideas. He tilted his torso to the side to create suspense, and then leaned backward with disbelief when she said something funny. The coup de grâce was when he'd come forward, ever so gently, to win a point. Still, he annoyed her by the liberty he took in criticizing the States.

Aroused, Lexi challenged him. "Are things here so much better?"

"You think I'm being cocky?"

"Yeah. Perhaps."

"It was different growing up in a British colony. Feeling inferior to the English. Kowtowing to foreign teachers. Not to mention the physical punishment."

"I'm sorry."

"My parents never talked much about their youth. But I spent a lot of time with my grandfather when he was dying, and heard many of his stories. He wanted me to know how lucky I was to be in Hong Kong. He believed my life would be brighter than his. Once he described a sign he walked by every day as a child. It was on the grass at the Hong Kong Cricket Club and it said, 'No dogs or Chinese allowed.'"

"How awful."

"I suppose knowing about his pain made me tougher." With zeal, Zheng added, "But what bothers me even more is how my own people's traditions are changing now. In some cases, being lost."

"What can you do?" Lexi asked.

"Tomorrow I will go feed my ancestors."

"I beg your pardon. Ancestors? You mean people who aren't living?" She thought his usage might differ from hers.

"Yes. It's called Ching Ming. A festival. People take food and money to family grave sites. Ours is on the mountainside. Would you like to see it?"

"I'd love to. But would that be an intrusion?"

"Oh, no. It's become very popular for others to attend. They're curious. We don't mind."

Lexi met Zheng early Saturday morning at the Star Ferry landing, and they headed up and over Hong Kong's spine in his two-seater Mercedes SL 450. The route was less populated and greener than any part of the island she'd seen so far. Lexi let the views enter her eyes and seep down to her toes. From the deep leather seat of Zheng's open convertible, her body swayed as they zigzagged up the Rock.

Traffic slowed to a standstill as they approached the grave sites. Like others, they parked on the outskirts. Everyone made the pilgrimage early in the morning and, together, they hiked in, five or more people abreast. Lexi loved seeing so many families in one place and in all kinds of dress. She was partial to the older women with brown, wizened faces and fierce eyes. In almost all instances, they had babies in tow and either guided them by the hand or strapped them onto their small, curved backs. Some children were dressed in finery, others sported T-shirts and jeans. Lexi marveled at the food the families brought: each had a basket filled with dozens of small, colored cakes that were unlike anything she'd seen in shop windows, or restaurants, or homes.

As their group approached the first rung of graves, people splintered off. When the crowd thinned out, Lexi concentrated on the smoky clouds of incense, thick in patches. Her eyes followed a pair of yellow joss sticks to one grave. An elderly woman knelt before the grave, holding the stick of incense vertically in front of her nose. Paying homage to her ancestors, she bowed. As she prayed, her body rocked from her head to her knees; she was lost in her thoughts as her torso fanned the smoke in all directions.

Zheng caught Lexi's eye and drew her back. Up the mountainside they climbed. Feeling lucky to be part of such an important rite of spring, Lexi celebrated every aspect. The climb. The colors. The faces. So many beautiful expressions. So much kinetic energy. And she knew she was only skimming the surface.

"Over here," Zheng said, as they were almost at the top.

He veered off the worn path, and she followed him around a stand of white flowering trees to a spectacular grave site. The burial places were carefully spread out under the treetops, giving each ancestor an uncommon amount of shade.

"These are the graves of my grandparents," he said. "My sisters will bring my little brothers later. Everyone must come. Especially since my parents are away. We have to represent the whole family."

Lexi saw a different man today, almost the opposite of the one the night before, who could intimidate with his erudition and quick mind. Fascinated, she watched Zheng open his backpack. He, too, had multicolored cakes and a circle of joss sticks. Then she saw the wads and wads of paper money. First he tenderly arranged the cakes. They knitted the grave sites together, up and down the side of the mountain. Lexi wouldn't have thought to do it that way, but it was perfect.

Bringing her closer to the ritual, he said, "Now I'm going to kneel and talk to my ancestors for a moment. Then I will light the incense and burn the money."

"Please don't let me interrupt," Lexi said softly.

"I'm happy you're here," he said, then turned to his responsibilities.

When it was time to leave, Lexi was exhilarated. Was it Zheng? Or had something changed in her? Her body quivered and she enjoyed the rush of new sensations. As an observer at Zheng's ancestors' graves, she'd merely witnessed an age-old ritual. Nonetheless, she intuited so much more. Lexi's premonition that she and Zheng had many others things to share was like a bridge that connected them in a mysterious manner.

Halfway down the mountainside, Zheng reached for her hand. Struck by how warm it was, she felt more than his skin and his fleshy palm. To Lexi, it was like a pillow. That was the moment when everything changed. They were together in a new way, and she trusted him.

Zheng drove her all over the island, then out to the peninsula known as the New Territories, taking the tunnel under
Hong Kong Harbor. The New Territories were still rural,
although new settlements were cropping up. Zheng parked the
car at the edge of a high bluff overlooking the water, and they
walked hand in hand along the side of the cliff. She breathed in
this new side of China, and could see and grasp so many contrasts: the South China Sea way below the craggy bluffs, and
the stretch of open space in an otherwise overpopulated patch
of the world. This was a land that encompassed virtually everything, and she was at peace here.

It felt good to slip into an intimate restaurant for dinner after
spending the afternoon outdoors. Zheng spoke to the waiter,
and the two of them engaged in a spirited conversation about
the menu.

Before she had finished her beer, the food started to come.
Frogs' legs. Eel soup. Stir-fried crab. Peking duck. And, at the
end, sweet almond soup. They laughed and talked easily
through the five courses. When Zheng asked her if she wanted
to see his place, every muscle and meridian in Lexi's body could
honestly say yes. She was exuberant as they made their way
back to Hong Kong island.

Her curiosity grew when the rosewood-paneled elevator
door in his building opened. They exited at the thirtieth floor
and, as if in a trance, she walked toward a black coramandel
screen in the hallway. She wanted to run her hands over the
mother-of-pearl people who appeared in all states of repose.
She loved the way they warmed the mountainside of the vast
Chinese landscape, all so demure against the vivid green and
black five-panel-wide backdrop.

"Magnificent," she said breathlessly.

"I could take you to workshops to see how they're made,"
Zheng said.

"Really?"

"Sure. This is an old one. But the new ones have their own fresh beauty."

"I can imagine."

With his hand on her shoulder, she felt a slight pressure as they stopped in front of a red lacquer door.

"Wow. What a color."

"It's for luck. And happiness. You know, brides in China are married in red dresses."

"Well, that's sort of what it means in the States. Passion. Risk." Laughing, Lexi added, "We resist it, though, and marry in white dresses."

"Then we're lucky to be here, not there," he said smoothly as he opened the tall, heavy, eight-foot door. "Welcome to my home."

Lexi walked in and her eyes settled on the dark brown, carved opium bed in the foyer. She noticed the multicolored Indian silk pillows with tiny hand-sewn mirrors that were fanned out under an enormous mirror centered over the bed.

As she walked up close, ready to touch the mirror, Zheng said, "It's feng shui."

She tilted her head, as if to ask for clarification.

"It's about connecting heaven and earth," he continued. "It's our way of creating a sanctuary. Evil spirits can't get in. The mirror deflects them."

"Incredible," she said, her eyes moving from one spot to the next. "But isn't this an opium bed? I've seen them in design shops at home."

"Yes. The Chinese used opium to help people get through grueling times. Especially artists. And for opera stars it turned out to have a purpose. It gave them soft, low voices."

"Come on." Her voice trailed off as she took in the splendor of the living room, a huge space where forty people could gather for drinks.

Arms around each other, they walked slowly toward a wall hung with art objects. She moved her hand around his black T-shirt and enjoyed the feel of his taut abs. "Tell me more."

"The buffet is from the T'ang dynasty, or sixth century," he said. "These are musical instruments that were once part of my mother's collection. This is the one I play."

Lexi looked curiously at the cluster of bamboo cylinders.

"It's a sheng, a mouth organ. It can reproduce the entire musical scale."

"It's wild," she said.

"Yes. It's shaped like the phoenix."

"The bird?"

"It was first seen at the birth of Confucius. According to the legend, it only appears when order reigns in a kingdom."

"And now?"

"No reports of one this century," he said, laughing. "But we're still looking."

Zheng picked up the sheng and cupped it in his hands. He turned toward Lexi and looked deeply into her eyes as he breathed in and out of the bamboo pipes. Lexi felt her body soften as the gentle, elusive tones of the music caressed her.

As he brought the ode to a languid close, she caught herself letting out a deep sigh, and asked, "Is there more?"

"Much more." Zheng planted his hand softly but firmly around hers. Lexi shivered. It felt as though his hand had always been part of her body. Zheng guided her to a small cabinet next to the side of the large picture window, and opened its delicate doors. She was dazzled by the glow of many small objects on the five glass shelves of the well-lighted cabinet.

"My father's collection of finger jade," Zheng said. As she took in the gentle features of his quiet face, he ever so slightly squeezed her hand.

She felt as if she was floating. It was all so beautiful. The sensual shapes. The charming stories. Zheng's body.

"What is the purpose of finger jade?"

"Now, that's a tough question. Depends on how old a person you ask. To my father, it was everything. Peace of mind. A kind of health bordering on immortality."

"Really?"

"Yeah. But when I was young, I thought it was awful. He was consumed by it."

"What do you mean?"

"Well, for starters, he wore a bag of them around his neck."

"You're not serious."

"Yes. They're like Chinese men's jewels. He could have hung them from his belt, the way others did. But he kept them by his heart. And played with them all the time."

"Played with them?"

"Sure. Try it. It's really kind of hypnotic." Zheng motioned for Lexi to pick one.

Peering in the cabinet, Lexi first noticed all the colors: green, gray, coral, white. There were fewer white ones and that intrigued her. Her eyes lit on a beautiful white oval, and easing the piece off the shelf, she felt its raised edges. Bringing it up to her eyes, Lexi saw the outline of two animals—dogs, in fact. The image formed a circle around the top of the finger jade. It was hard to see where and how their bodies joined. Then it came to her. The union. The head of each dog met the tail of its mate. Like a garland.

She rubbed her thumb around the oval. "It's magnificent," she said in hushed tones.

"They also ward off evil spirits. But mostly people like to rub and pat them for tactile pleasure."

"Show me."

Zheng's head turned down to the side, eyes bright and he picked one. "This is a ts'ung," he said. "It represents the earth deity. It was once part of a dagger."

"Let me feel it." Fascinated by the shape of the hollow cylinder enclosed in a rectangular body, she was reminded of male and female parts. Bound together, like ancient symbols.

She returned it to him gently, and gave him a coy look. As he began to stroke the ts'ung, he said, "People think that when you touch the jade, you bring it alive." His smile broadened, ever so slightly. The biggest smile since they arrived at his apartment.

Lexi grinned, sensing that Zheng could make her feel vital. How she wished he were moving his hands over and around her body—just like that. Slowly, tenderly. With just the right pressure.

As she watched him rub the jade, she paid attention to his hand. Smaller than the hands of most men she knew. But better in so many ways. More knowing. More certain. Controlled, but free. She was intoxicated. Her eyes carved out a route from his face, so relaxed and expressionless, to the tender muscles of his forearm.

With the jade resting in his open palm, all of his fingers worked the piece. While she could barely detect the tree-shaped veins below his wrist, she slavishly watched the small muscles next to them move up and down.

He must have noticed the gaze. With eyes boring into hers, he asked, "Have you had enough?"

"Yes," she whispered. "For now, anyway."

He slowly turned his body and moved toward the cabinet. He placed the ts' ung back on its glass shelf. It was alive, well tended, and back home—perhaps even savoring the memory. Zheng put his arm around her waist and let it ride up to her breast as they walked toward the picture window. Hong Kong was aglow. Tiny white lights cascaded down the peak and a big, bold neon rim trimmed out the harbor—all in all, an electrified dragon.

Lexi felt Zheng's hand move in toward her breast, and she followed its arc. As she turned to face him, he reached for her shoulder. Like braided flowers, her arms made a circle around his neck, and their lips joined easily, as tender as lotus blossoms. All at once, they had a perfect bond. They were just like the dogs at play on the ivory jade.

"Shall we make ourselves more comfortable?" Zheng asked. "Down the hall, perhaps?"

"And be more intimate?"

"If you like."

"I've grown fond of you so quickly," Lexi said. "But it's been such a big day."

"We could just hold each other."

"That would be enough?"

Pulling his head back a few inches to look clearly into her eyes, he whispered, "Why not?"

Zheng guided Lexi to his bedroom, an exotic interior dressed in smoke mirrors and black lacquer, with myriad ancient objects scattered about. Lexi's attraction to Zheng grew as she looked around the room. What a sensitive, unusual man had come her way. Feeling mellow, even hopeful, she wanted to make love to him, and knew that tomorrow would be just right. The bed was covered in beige silk. Bathed by all of her senses, she felt a rush of well-being. A mixture of contentment and wonder. What rich dreams she'd conjure up tonight.

Lexi got into bed and closed her eyes as she felt Zheng's arms around her. This was maybe the closest she'd been in a long time to satisfied desire. Was this what Asia was all about? An eroticism that slowly, yet constantly, takes you somewhere new? Takes you so far that you don't think to look back for hours at a time.

Before dozing off, she visualized all that happened to her today. Grave sites. Frogs' legs. Opium beds. Mouth organs. Finger jade. She'd toyed with antiquities that could have been in an exhibition, but were part of someone's life. The beauty and wonder of all she'd seen embraced her soul, along with an uncanny desire to surrender. Totally. And she had. She just didn't know when she'd submitted, and never would have thought to question why. Or to what.

When Lexi awoke to the smell of strong coffee, she struggled to make sense of her surroundings. As her early morning confusion receded, she was pleased to notice that her jet lag was finally gone. Stretching her heels toward the bottom of the bed, she felt good.

Then the images started to filter through her mind and she reran her personal video of Hong Kong. Multicolored cakes for the dead. Paper money for Zheng's ancestors to spend in the afterlife. The spectacular views of China from the New Territories. Zheng's finger on that jade. Lexi was blown away by twenty-four hours of Asian experiences.

The best, though, was Zheng's supple body. His catlike moves and intuitive hands seemed to deconstruct sensuality. First one body part. Then another. One muscle group. Then the next. What would it feel like all rolled up?

Lexi thought about that as she watched the light filter through the thick blinds. She was eager to take a closer look at Zheng's bedroom by day. As she stretched out on her side, Zheng opened the door. He was carrying a gold lacquer breakfast tray. First she noticed the coffeepot, sugar and creamer, then her eyes went to the vase. The peach blossoms that were set so delicately on three tender branches cast an erotic spell.

"Good morning," he said with a smile. "Lexi, I'm sorry I wasn't here when you woke up. Ching would have brought this in, but I thought it might be more comfortable for you if I got it myself."

As he raised the shades of the two windows, she watched daylight wash his face. His eyes were dark, but they flickered with a quiet light whenever he spoke.

This morning, Zheng wore a black silk robe with the kind of geometric print common on ascots. Tied tightly at the waist, his garb accentuated the bold contrast between his wide shoulders and his slim hips. Moving with assurance, he lit the room in stages, starting first with the window, then stopping next to her at the bedside table to turn on a light made from a porcelain vase.

"What a gorgeous combination." She gestured to the lamp's base. "Sort of purply red. Red for passion and blue for spirit."

"That's the sang-de-boeuf glaze," he said. "Ox blood. What's also unique is that the glaze tends to flow as it's fired in the kiln. That's why the neck is white."

The image was arousing. She looked up at the neck of the vase. Blood-running hot is what she'd call it, and hers was definitely simmering. The changes were subtle, like a kiln heating. Stoked with desire, Lexi thought of her flesh as warm, pink clay, ready to be transformed—at high temperatures—into a piece of art. She felt radiant.

Lexi sipped her coffee and sampled Hong Kong's version of western pastry. She sensed her affair with Zheng was taking on a more elaborate cast. Rituals like these sustain relationships, Lexi thought. Then, just as quickly, she chased away the sentiment. What she liked was this simple way of being together. When the last mango slice disappeared from the plate, Lexi saw Zheng's face soften.

"With all those bed covers, I can hardly see you," he said as his hand stroked hers.

"We should do something about that," she said.

First he stroked her body under the thick comforter. As his hands touched her breast, Lexi arched her back to give more of herself. She tingled, inside and out. Her breasts, so full at this stage of her cycle, begged for the attention. Perhaps he'd tend to them with the same delicacy with which he ate the peeled mango. Ate the thick yellow flesh right from his hand. Yes. She liked the way Zheng's warm hand petted, then squeezed her. As his thumb played with her hard nipple, she felt a rush and reached toward him with her lips. Opening her mouth slightly, she welcomed his tongue. He played so freely, then took the liberty to move on. When he cupped her crotch, she relaxed and waited for the rapture. Now she was all his.

As Zheng tossed off the bed covers, Lexi wished the camisole she was wearing would vanish on its own. He pulled her panties down. Lexi took charge of her camisole. Tilting her head down, she trusted him with her breasts. In an instant, she was naked. More than that, she felt beautiful as she caught her reflection in his wide eyes.

"Oh, Lexi," he whispered, as his mouth descended to her nipples. His tongue. His hands. His whole body moving in on her. She stretched back on the bolster pillow, warmed by the morning sun. Her legs moved lower down the bed. And her knees opened wide.

Stroking his flesh as he moved on top of her, she surrendered to the kaleidoscope of sensations, her eyes taking in what her skin might miss. Lexi's mind was hitched to every millimeter he touched. She closed her eyelids as Zheng, nearly out of sight, kissed her belly, then moved his body between her legs. Breathing deeply and in sync with each caress, she could feel her vagina pulse. What would he do first? Touch her? Lick her? Whisper? Ask permission? Or merely plant himself, and listen?

As his lips brushed over her pubic hair, her pelvis tensed up. She wanted it all. No need to take it in stages. He must have understood. From her wet, wet labia. To her electric thighs. Past the early, earthy moans of anticipation.

All at once his finger slid deep into her vagina while his teeth smoothed, then nipped her clitoris. She cried out in surprise as he gently bit her, then lost focus when his finger moved so deep into her body. Is that when it happened? Or was it the sucking? Or the pressure of his lips? Or the finger that tickled her anus? Unable to discriminate, Lexi gave herself over to the whirl of sensations.

In moments, her orgasms started. As did the cries of disbelief. Of thankfulness. Of incredulity. How could a man make her come so quickly? Give so fully?

His sable tongue wouldn't let her go. Round and round. Over and over. His pace picked up as her fluids of joy started to roll. Her laughter mimicked the tiny eruptions, rollicking at first, then loud, as her clit caught fire.

"Oh, Zheng, let me touch you," she cried, grasping for a conscious thought.

"Not yet, Lexi.

"No?"

"No. You'll see."

Giving her time to revel in the many sensations, he kissed one inner thigh. Then the other. She slowed down her breathing as his hand gripped the ball of her foot. Then the other one. A deep massage. More currents of electricity running through her body. As Zheng got up on his knees, she saw his hard cock for the first time. Just when her mouth eased into a smile, he grinned, too.

Locked in the gaze, Lexi took him into her heart. She ached as she watched him stroke his cock. He looked so powerful. In her mind's eye, the image of his cock was like a tulip. She saw his manliness everywhere, and she sensed his intent even before he moved. Oozing, her vagina reached out.

He knelt down and gave her the thrust she wanted. Once inside, he stopped. Everything stopped, even her breath. Still. Completely still. Lexi gasped at first, then her throbbing vagina started to let go. How extraordinary. How complete. Now all that registered was the unity.

"I want you to feel all of me," Zheng said. "The way I have tasted all of you." Gently moving her to the side, he continued, "We have plenty of time. Trust me."

And Lexi did. At first she'd wanted more, right away, but now she was locked in the mystery of his words and his plan. The encounter took on new proportions, and the suspense piqued her senses. She had so much to unravel. To feel. Moment by moment. She loved the way he stayed inside her and they just cuddled. And on her side, she felt the full weight of his cock.

Lexi was nearly in a trance when he whispered, "We'll just stay still now."

Lexi liked the way he slowly moved inside her. Her vaginal walls no longer throbbed; they quivered. That was okay. She could feel him ease over each ripple of her vaginal wall. Leisurely. Then Lexi moved into another realm, and time stopped.

Lexi let Zheng take the lead, but felt the involuntary trembling inside her vagina. Then she wiggled a bit, but couldn't shake the feeling. The sense that they were one entity. Like two horses tethered together. Not yet. But she had an inkling.

In any case, it was a feast. She felt things she'd never felt before with a man. Trust. Hope. Care. Yes, he would take care of her. Her feelings. Her body. She didn't know about the soul just yet. She'd felt a lot of confusion about that, but things were changing.

Each whisper reverberated. Some went deeper still. Lexi started to giggle as it all hit. How he'd just given her this time and his attention. She felt like she mattered more to him than she ever had to others. How simple, yet how extraordinary. It had never happened this way before. What could she give him in return?

"How are you doing?" Zheng whispered.

"Great. It's so erotic. Like everything in your place."

"Good," he murmured. "Why don't you turn on your stomach now? Let's see if I can convince you that our Tao knows more than *Cosmo* about what you call the G spot."

"You're so funny," she said. "This is unbelievable."

She would have done anything he asked. On her stomach, she waited for his next move, and as his finger climbed up inside her vagina, she let her mind go. Breathing from her diaphragm to counter the pressure, she basked in the swells. Whatever it was, it worked. The sensations. The movement. Slowly she rocked her pelvis to be part of the process. Soft moans. Sheer surrender. All the sensations seemed new. Soon she was a babe bathing in her own waters.

"Come up a bit," he said, gently touching her knee as he slid his hand from within her.

On her knees with her buttocks facing her eager, new lover, Lexi felt Zheng tuck into her vagina, replaying all the sensations with more speed. Her orgasms broke again as he pounded against her buttocks.

"Okay. Okay," he whispered feverishly. She felt the firm pressure of his hand on her waist and she paused. Feeling him withdraw, she laid down to stretch, just as his hand squeezed her shoulder. Another pause.

On her back now, she was awed by the gentle way he knelt above her. Her mouth leapt for his cock, as she pulled him closer by his buttocks. Her hands squeezed one cheek, then the other. She pulled him deeper and deeper into her throat and set a fast pace. Her finger edged into the crack of Zheng's behind, just as her lips tightened their grip.

"Not yet, Lexi. Not yet," he muttered with sounds that hardly formed words.

Then Zheng pulled back, and Lexi struggled to bring him into focus. He let out a cry as he pierced her to the core in a final round. Whether the Rock moved or she merely imagined it in motion, Lexi didn't know. She was pure sensation. Totally consumed, and willing to devour. To ravage him in any way she could.

Passionate, Lexi gripped Zheng's shoulders and let her mind focus on the stream of sensations. He went deeper, and was as hard as ivory. Allowing herself to lose control, she heaved recklessly. Her tender flesh burned, and when the boundaries between his body and hers collapsed, Lexi, too, gave way. Lexi realized she had all there was to have. That her sensuality was her gift.

They showered. And nuzzled. And teasingly stroked each other's wet bodies in the majesty of his grey marble shower. She would never lose touch with that moment. Lexi's mind was awash in revelation, in the discovery of her completeness. The way she had gotten there, and the need to keep the knowledge alive inside her. Hong Kong fed her senses, then unleashed her imagination. She'd been open to the exploration and now had her chip of the Rock. Her piece of jade.

Over the next four days, Lexi and Zheng were in another world. It was as though they had always been together and would be forever. Neither of them wanted to talk about Saturday, when Lexi was to leave for the States.

Lexi headed to Zheng's on Friday not knowing how different their last night would be from their first. They'd come together quickly, and had much in common. The anguish of heading home so soon made Lexi want to bargain for more time. But she knew her fantasy was foolish. In every way, they were worlds apart.

Zheng's driver picked her up at work, as usual. Only a week had passed since they had met and, already, they had so many rituals. Lexi walked through the red lacquer door to Zheng's apartment—a place she'd started to think of as home. She stopped mid-stride. Zheng had lit it all with candles. The foyer. The living room. She wondered what the bedroom looked like.

He was waiting for her in the living room, amid the candles. Stunned to see his apartment cast in a romantic Western glow, Lexi wondered what else Zheng had in mind to make her last night special. She locked her eyes on his as he walked quickly toward her. Sensing a difference, she took in more details. Dressed in his robin's egg blue jeans and grey Armani shirt with its subtle, sensuous threads, Lexi was struck by how much he looked like a model in a *Times* fashion issue.

In just one week, she'd learned how deftly Zheng could cast a spell on her. He'd intoxicated her with his sophistication at Mary's party, then charmed her with his tender devotion to his family at the Ching Ming festival. As her lover, she couldn't have wished for more. But the intensity in his eyes sent another, perhaps darker message now.

Lexi's shoulders tensed and she felt clumsy when he kissed her. Unable to meet his lips with the same urgency she felt as he gripped her, Lexi felt shy around Zheng for the first time.

He seemed to sense her unease and grew unusually animated. He poured the French champagne into the thin Baccarat crystal glasses and maneuvered her with finesse around the living room, waltzing to classical music.

Squeezing her hand as he twirled her about, he whispered, "I imagined something like this when I first saw you."

"Dancing?"

"Yes, actually."

"You're so romantic."

"And you?"

"A not-so-tough businesswoman, I suppose."

"And the love of ..."

"A willing accomplice," she mustered as her hand went limp.

As if aware of her sadness, Zheng took a lighter tact.

"I remember the spark in your eyes that first night, when I was critical of the States. You snapped at me, and I was afraid you might bite."

"A regular American pit bull."

"Blue ribbon."

"What I remember," Lexi said, teasing, "was how I thought you needed more control than I could give up."

"I've been off balance ever since."

"Guess I did okay," she said, feeling more playful.

"Do," he insisted, then caught himself, adding gently, "I have a gift for you."

"You've been a gift," she said.

Zheng gave her a sharp look at her use of the past tense.

"It's over here. See if you can spot it," he said, composing himself.

Taken aback, Lexi followed as he walked toward the picture window, stopping at the lighted cabinet.

Lexi laughed when she spotted the ivory finger jade, tied with a fat red ribbon.

"No, Zheng," she said, hesitating. "I couldn't."

"You must."

She stilled her body and her eyes welled with tears.

"How can you be sad looking head on at the two of us?" he said, as he reached in the cabinet and lifted the ivory nugget.

Lexi rubbed the jade, stroking it softly around the edges of the puffy bow. The two carved dogs chasing each other around the border of the finger jade did capture the time they had spent together. Zheng was right to be annoyed with Lexi viewing their relationship in the past tense.

Lexi tried to quell her uneasiness. Or perhaps to right her wrong. "Zheng," she said, rubbing the jade, "this is magnificent. Do you think the artist imagined us together?"

"In a dream, perhaps. I like the fact that it doesn't change."

"Shall I keep it in my pocket, or wear it on a chain near my heart like your father?"

"As you like," he said, dropping his eyes to her breast.

"Thank you," she said, kissing him tenderly, like a brother.

"We're having dinner here. And I have another surprise for the Jacuzzi. Let's go there now."

Perched above some of the most spectacular landscape in the world, they sat in warm, bubbly water. Lexi merged with the million twinkling lights just outside her reach and felt terrific. But a feeling in her gut sliced through the fantasy. This felt as perfect as a fairy tale, but somehow it was his, not hers.

"It's as though we have it all," he said, subdued by the champagne and pleased that his preparations had gone so well.

"This is wonderful," she said softly.

"At first I thought I was happy because of you. Then I realized it's us."

"Yes," she said noncommittally.

"We can go anywhere together. We could be a great force in Asia."

"You're very lucky. You have the backing of a family fortune."

"We can do it together, Lexi."

"Oh, Zheng," she said as her voice dropped, registering a note of doubt.

"Why not? It doesn't matter that you're not Chinese. People think globally now."

"It's not that."

"Then it's me? My background?"

"Of course not."

"Lexi, I wish I understood you better. Do you know what you want?"

"Something is changing in me. And it's good."

"Love does that."

"But it's still confusing."

"Only if you're afraid."

Lexi wondered if that was the problem.

"Can you do your job from here?" he asked. "I've got a better idea. You could start your own production company. I can back you financially."

"Starting a venture is more like two jobs. Mine's full-time and a half as it is, and I wish it were a lot less intense."

"Are you playing hard to get?" he asked in his mock Brooklyn accent.

"Please."

"You're sleepy?"

"No. Not sleepy. I'm sad."

"Lexi, I love you. Stay here with me."

"Oh, Zheng. I feel so much love for you, but ..."

"Lexi, take the time you need."

"This is a wonderful life, but it's your life."

"Lexi, you said . . ."

"I've felt many things here. It's been so long . . ."

"Look at me," Zheng said, urgently clasping her face between his palms. "This is real. Right now. Don't be afraid."

"I'm not."

"Then what?"

"Worse."

"Is someone waiting for you?"

"No. I'm waiting for me."

He laughed. "We'll wait together."

"Seriously. Would you leave your world for me? Come back to Boston? Live a simpler life?"

Zheng was incredulous. "You *love* Hong Kong."

"Boston is my life. That's what I want."

"Perhaps I misjudged you."

"If I can't balance my life there, I certainly can't do it here. I'd be seduced by the extravagance." Mustering more energy, she said, "You're going somewhere I've already been. All that power. All that duty. All those people."

"Been?"

"Well, not in the same way. Not in such a big way. But similar dance steps."

"You're losing me."

"All that drive and ambition may make sense for you. But not for me."

"What do you need?"

"I'm just figuring that out."

Lexi smiled before disappearing under the water and coming up between Zheng's legs.

Yes, she thought, as she awoke early the next morning, her last day in Hong Kong. She and Zheng shared one dream. The one about passion. And they sure knew how to make it real. But as she turned to her side and tucked her knees up to her chest, she knew her instinct was right. They were great as lovers, but she needed something more.

Hopeful, she believed that her imagination had started

dredging up images from her soul, desires that were going to take her in a new direction. She wanted her outer world to mirror her inner world. Slowing down was part of that process.

She was tentative during breakfast, as was he. It was hard to be together for what might be the last time. For Lexi, everything was painful because it was all mixed up. Her ears still burned with desire when she heard his voice, and it was harder than ever to take her eyes off his hands, which had come to mean so much. Small. Smooth. Skin stretched tight, as if to keep so much power inside.

The rest of the parting rituals happened mostly by rote. Lexi managed them in a blur. All of her energies leapt ahead of her heart. The fear did that. An entire relationship woven from the moment by two people who had a knack for being spontaneous. Now they were frozen. After all this, what was left? Then the floodgate of their terror broke.

"Oh, Lexi. I wish we didn't come from such distant places."

"Don't say that. That's why I love you. And why I'll remember everything about you."

Then they loved each other's bodies, honoring what was special between them with adoration, passion.

Lexi wondered if she sobbed all the way back to her hotel because she'd seen the tears in Zheng's eyes, or because she thought she'd made the wrong decision. She cried off and on during her twenty-one-hour flight to Boston. But by the time she headed into work on Monday, her healing had begun.

She was more hopeful about relationships now, and knew she could create a caring bond with someone special. Though it had to be more than a good connection. She needed something that went deeper. Zheng loved the glitz of the heady world he lived in. He seemed most comfortable mixing with high-powered social figures. She imagined him queing up to meet statesmen or royalty across the globe. Zheng still needed the trappings and toys of a rich young man, and perhaps he always would.

Turning over the bittersweet memories as she drove into work, Lexi looked forward to getting back to her desk. Smiling as she swung open the large mahogany doors of Bradford's corporate office, Lexi wondered if the place would seem changed because she herself was different. The white snapdragons waiting on her desk, a gift from Rose, brought to mind the ritual she shared with Zheng at the cemetery. How many other things would dull her heart before she was totally healed?

After a brisk greeting, Rose said, "Mr. Hockhauser has scheduled a meeting with you, Louis, and Mr. Bryant."

Louis looked in a bit before ten and gave her a smile. "Nice," he said, noting the snap dragons. "Rose brought me a bottle of Jack Daniels to open after the meeting. I guess I look more stressed out than you."

Louis waited with her for Hockhauser to summon them. Lexi was grateful for Louis's friendship. Somewhat removed, as a lawyer, from the guts of the business issues, Louis nevertheless brought expertise that complemented her deep knowledge of markets, strategies, and opportunities. The real bond they shared was their secret language. Grunts. Buzzwords. Gestures. Communication was stripped down to its essence when the two of them talked. Her friendship with Shakti was similar, she mused. Good friends needed only a few sounds to travel great distances towards each other. Could lovers also share a muted bond?

Lexi thought often about Zheng. They had spoken more than once since she'd left Hong Kong. She knew how much she cared for him, and God knows she felt he had been implanted in her head. Occasionally he would push her just a little to

reconsider a future with him. He did not yet entirely understand her need to let go and search for a relationship that would
feed her equilibrium. Right now, Lexi needed to slow down
enough to let those images that sprang from her soul guide her
life. Only that could make her whole.

Lexi's comfort with her decision to let go of the relationship
with Zheng made it easier to love him as a friend. Once Shakti
had told her that in Hindu there are dozens of words for love,
since we can love so many people in different ways. Did one of
those dozens of words connote self-loving?

"Al wants to put together the final package on Starlight
today," Louis warned. "Price. Terms. Negotiating strategy. It's
been chaotic around here, Lexi. Things are moving very
quickly. Raymond Chou's been hounding Al. I just got new
drafts of the deal structure from outside counsel . . ."

"Good," she said, a bit nervous. Starlight's CEO was formida-
ble. "We have all the information to do it. We just need to get
a formal go-ahead from both sides."

"Nobody knows where Al is on this right now. There's a real
estate deal in the works that could short circuit this one," he
said carefully.

Their eyes rested on each other for another moment,
exchanging a full understanding of the morning that lay ahead.

She pulled out her Starlight file and skimmed once again the
summary description of the company, the key financial scenar-
ios, and her notes about issues Hockhauser had raised. She
visualized the meeting: he'd grill them, turn the tables, and get
himself and whomever else appeared vulnerable into a frenzy.
Lexi tried to relax her neck and shoulders and find a place inside
her where she could remain calm. Samurai calm. Centered.

"Good morning." Al Hockhauser's baritone seemed stereo-
phonic in the confines of the conference room as he walked

over to first shake hands with Lexi; then with Tom Bryant, the new financial officer; and finally with Louis.

Ever the gentleman in countless conventional ways, Al also had a charisma that made him endearing when he was in a good mood. Those who worked closely with him knew he could turn mean in seconds.

"Well, look who's back," Al exclaimed.

Lexi flashed Al a huge smile.

"She looks great, doesn't she?" Al said to no one in particular. "Must have agreed with you."

"It's a sensational part of the world. And the Chou brothers are terrific. We got a lot done," Lexi said, as she settled into a black leather chair in front of Al's desk.

Taking the lead, Al said, "We've been working on the Starlight deal for a while. My final question to all of you is, 'Can we make money by investing in this global venture, particularly with the start-up in Asia?' Lexi, why don't you start us off."

"Sure," Lexi said, swiveling her chair to the side as she focused her eyes on Al. "The potential is enormous. What I've done is look at current markets. Competitors. Emerging distribution technologies. Profitability. And get a feel for the type of programming the Starlight Group would want to buy."

Challenging her, Al asked, "Do we know what people in Asia want to watch?"

"This is new territory, Al. We have ideas. Lots of them. But we'll need to experiment," Lexi said, as she flicked back her hair.

"Sounds costly," Al countered, adjusting his tie.

"Not really," Lexi said, looking at Louis and Bob as she spoke. "We'll lead with mainstream movies, mostly U.S. stuff. Asian sports. Kids' programming."

"Bradford doesn't need big losses right now," Al said sharply, addressing the whole group.

"Al, the reason we've invested in new technologies is the upside. Satellite television can be a sweetener for Bradford Communications," Lexi said, as she leaned forward.

"This has to work, Lexi," Al said.

"We'll put in twenty million to start. Then re-evaluate the project in twelve months," Lexi responded, swiveling her chair toward Louis.

"Does the deal stand if we take the most likely scenario for the U.S. and Europe, plus dollars from the worst case Asian scenario?" Louis interrupted.

"Yes," Bob said. "Based solely on the financials."

"What makes you so sure about this, Lexi?" Al said, tapping his Mont Blanc pen lightly on his desk blotter.

"The Starlight Channel will be the first satellite channel in each of the five Asian cities. That's key to our strategy. And there's no competition from other program distributors like cable television."

Looking at Louis and Lexi, Al asked, "Are you both on board?"

"Yes," said Louis.

Lexi reveled in the moment. It was another good reason to have left Hong Kong and Zheng. Her friends were here. Her life, her work, and, scant as it might be, her personal self felt grounded here. The knot inside her loosened another inch. She was glad to be home.

Bob had picked up where Louis left off. "There's enough cash flow from the European operations to cover the start-up in Asia.

"I'll call the Chous and tell them it's a go," Al said, as his lips widened into a faint smile.

Ebullient, Lexi headed back to her office. Whenever she won some ground in a negotiation with Al, Lexi felt a charge run through her body. Her senses were sharper and her spirit soared. It happened when she accessed, then released her passion for a project, and the effect was addictive. Lexi's phone rang as she reached her desk.

"Lexi," Al's voice rang out, "let me be the first to commend you. I decided to do the deal after I read your memo last week. You did a great job on the financials. Just wanted to get everybody on the same page this morning."

Somewhat surprised, Lexi said, "Thanks, Al. I appreciate the support."

"You're the right person to get this off the ground, Lexi. Represent our interests in the partnership. Live in Hong Kong for a while."

"That's a big vote of confidence, Al." Lexi said slowly. "But I'm afraid it's out of the question."

"Are you listening?" Al asked irritably. "This is your lucky break." Then, in a gentler voice, "I'm putting you in charge of operations. Co-president of the venture."

"That would be an honor, but I can't do it," Lexi said quietly.

"Of course you can," Al said. "It's your best career move."

"I need to stay settled now. Simplify things," Lexi said.

"This is what I've been training you for!"

"It's not about you, Al," Lexi said.

"It makes me wonder if we should do the deal at all," he bellowed.

Al had a way of pushing her buttons. This had never been so clear to her before. The pain involved in leaving Hong Kong had opened many doors in Lexi's mind. Exasperated, she said in a hoarse whisper, "I have to pull my personal life together."

"Oh," Al mumbled, clearly a bit flustered.

"There's nothing in particular going on, but ..."

"I hadn't heard about the new guy," Al said, cutting in. "To be honest, Lexi, I've always wondered about that."

"There is no guy," she said.

Al's tone softened and Lexi sensed he was sorry for leaning on her. "You know, Lexi," he said, clearing his throat, "I remember when you first began working here, right after your divorce. I've watched you blossom." He hesitated. "I guess I feel somewhat proprietary about your career. No—more than that. I've watched you mature. Maybe I feel a little bit like a father." Hockhauser was not known for sensitivity toward his employees. Lexi was astounded by the intimacy of this conversation.

Touched by his gruff attempt to be personal, Lexi realized he was telling her he understood. That in his way he was granting her permission to open up her life and let in more than Bradford Communications. "Thanks, Al," she said. It seemed important not to underscore the unique moment that had passed between them. Al's expression of affection was special, fragile, and Lexi treasured it, and him. Yes. It was good to be home. After a long pause she said, "Brian Connors would be a great choice for Hong Kong."

"I'll think about that," he said with a calm voice. "And you'd work closely with him from here?"

"Of course."

Lexi hung up, feeling she'd been hit by a thunderbolt. She was surprised by Al's offer, and her instant rejection of it. But she knew she was right. Lexi had been thinking more and more about Shakti's advice since returning from Hong Kong. Yes. Shakti had guessed correctly. Lexi wanted to have a committed relationship and was willing to create more time to let her imagination conjure up the images that could lead the way. Her work was in the way. She couldn't let her work dominate her life right now.

Perhaps it was coincidence or synchronicity, but not fifteen minutes after her conversation with Al, Rose announced that Shakti was on the line.

"Hello, Lexi," Shakti said cheerfully. "Raj and I were talking last night about you. He and I had dinner with a partner in my firm who has just transferred here. Each of us had the same thought—that he would be perfect for you. Will you let me give him your telephone number? David Morgan. He's a great guy."

"How odd that you're calling about this now." Lexi quickly caught Shakti up on all that had happened since she'd left for Hong Kong, and though she was careful not to dwell on her feelings for Zheng, Shakti got the message.

"Sounds sexy. Guess I read your mind, huh?" Shakti said.

"Isn't that what friends do?" Lexi quipped. Then after a pause, "I'd like to meet him."

"Done."

"Are you going to tell me more?" Lexi asked.

"No. Don't need to. Just enjoy yourself."

Lexi said, "This is why I love you. We're so in sync."

"Exactly."

Lexi left the office early, her spirits much brighter than when she'd set out that morning. Stopping off at the gym, she breezed through her program with new vigor, starting with the treadmill. She felt the difference as soon as she pulled the bar behind her head and began her lat pull downs. Every muscle on her back came alive. She could imagine her warm blood as it pulsed, making microscopic ripples up and down her back. Her chest presses were more fluid and precise than usual. Slowly moving her arms toward the ceiling, she felt graceful and her torso opened wide.

Lexi lovingly worked her triceps before getting down on the floor to begin the mat work, finishing up with the three different ways she'd learned to tone her abs. The workout was like a meditation, and she could visualize locking Zheng away in a special chamber of her heart. What they had shared would be like her precious piece of finger jade, a nugget she could take out and toy with whenever she wanted to, for the rest of her life. Soon, she knew, it would be time to call him and bid him a proper adieu. The old-fashioned phrase fit her feelings.

She did not realize she was smiling until the man stretching on the mat next to her gave her a seductive look. Must be giving off loving vibes, she thought to herself. She rose, went to the women's locker room and lingered in the eucalyptus scent that filled the space.

Arriving home before dark, Lexi was happy to see the jonquils coming up in the beds around the edge of her red brick Georgian home. She stopped the car in the driveway and got out to sleuth her front yard for more signs of spring. The day lilies were inching up from the ground and she brushed them like feathers with her palm. The crocuses were standing proud, their tender stems bent slightly from recent rain. Lexi stooped down to smell the earth, the cradle of procreation. She ran her fingers through the soil, then brought the flowers to her nose to sniff the rebirth at hand.

Heading in the front door, she felt hopeful and impulsively ducked into the living room, turning on the tiny halogen ceiling lights before taking off her coat. Lexi surveyed the space and took stock of the changes she'd made in her home since Jake moved out. Gone were the pine antiques, as well as her handmade curtains. Slowly, she'd redecorated, opting for a sleek look rather than the homespun one she'd fashioned when her nesting instincts first hit. The soft sensuality of Italian design had won her heart. For Lexi, the most spectacular purchase was still the long, grey velvet sofa. She had fallen in love with the simple elegance of its subtle, slanted back. Next to it, she'd placed a round, faceted mahogany coffee table that was as beautiful as a curved wet river rock with a rich, blackish grain.

Glancing around the room, Lexi imagined the sheer pleasure of scrunching her toes deep in the plush, cayenne-red rug and spending the evening there.

Lately she'd been buying artwork, and as she turned to leave the room, her gaze stopped on the glass sculpture suspended from the ceiling in the far corner. She feasted her eyes on the folds of pale aqua slumped glass, caged artfully in a delicate container made of thin metal wire. She'd first seen Mary Shaffer's work at the Boston Museum of Fine Arts, and it had the same grace and sensuality that Georgia O'Keeffe's paintings conjured up. Titled *Evenfold*, the piece's subtle and suggestive lines were like ocean waves. Suspended from two butterfly bolts behind the ceiling, the sculpture moved ever so slightly with the air currents. Lexi had treated herself to the piece after her promotion, and took refuge in its inspiration.

After dinner she had a long chat with a friend in California. At nine, David called. Lexi was nervous when she heard the deep, resonant tone of his voice. She hadn't expected a call so soon.

"I have it on good authority that you are the most wonderful, available woman in Boston."

"Shakti loves me. But I hope she hasn't built me up too much. You'll be disappointed."

"Shakti doesn't strike me as someone prone to exaggeration."

While the conversation was light in tone, the feeling was extraordinary. He sounded kind and understanding. His speech was on the slow side. Won over by his patient way and quiet sense of humor, Lexi felt she'd been caressed by his voice. After they hung up, she lost herself again in the creamy texture of his words. They danced in her ears as she gazed at the even waves of her glass sculpture. She felt grateful.

Lexi had suggested lunch. Though David seemed disappointed, he'd handled it well. Sounding personable, he said gently, "I don't know about you, but lunches are a disaster for me."

So dinner it was, but she drew the line at Sunday night. To Lexi it sounded almost as safe as lunch. To David it was dinner, not lunch. Savvy enough not to build undue expectations, she wanted to come out of the gate with composure. Picking up speed later was never a problem.

Sunday evening came quickly, and Lexi put behind her the morass of meetings, issues, and follow-up projects that racked her week. The question of what to wear was paramount. She spun around in her closet and began pulling clothes off the rod, uncertain of the image she wanted to create, or, for that matter, to avoid.

Bright colored skirts looked like tight colored skirts. There was the fraudulence of sheer blouses. The put-on of high boots. Black looked pseudo when juxtaposed to her soul. Finally, a form-fitting, gray textured designer's dress caught her eye. Cut on a bias, its subtle stripes joined at an angle in the front and the back, creating interest and a trim line. Sophisticated, yet minimal enough for a Sunday night, it was just right.

Lexi added a sheer black slip to show her lines to best advantage. Pausing in front of the mirror, she saw the reflection of an attractive, sexy woman that belied her long days at the office and lingering sadness over the forced parting with Zheng. There were still moments, like this one, when missing him made her feel like an empty shell.

One more round with the mirror. Lexi eased the end of the rat tail comb under the hair above her crown, hoping a little extra height would balance out the full-moon shape of her face. Even she could appreciate the way her clear green eyes sparkled. Thick, bow lips rested softly at the base of her face and looked as inviting as a mother's hug. A pair of muted silver earrings trimmed out the look. She gave herself a big smile, reached for the light switch, and moved down the stairs with zeal.

The ringing of the doorbell made her jittery. David wasted no time moving through the storm door. Once inside, he looked at her boldly. That was the moment Lexi replayed again and again, for months. The flash of light coming from his huge brown eyes. And that thick auburn hair that Shakti never mentioned. But what stoked Lexi's soul were his broad smile and sensuous lips. Thinking back months and even years later, she could never honestly be sure if it had been unadulterated lust and if so, whose it was, his or hers?

Noting hundreds of details, Lexi liked this new person and moved quickly through the steps of making someone comfortable in her home. Taking his khaki raincoat, she ushered him into her living room. For a moment everything else seemed small compared to his large frame and presence. He moved about the room with an energy she found intoxicating. As he turned to take in the entire space, his eyes focused on the closest wall.

He pointed to the painting and said, "My mother would love this."

This gave her reason to take a fresh look at the piece, an ancient Italian fresco. To Lexi, it spoke of time gone by. Memories of Jake. Lexi noted that the primitive beauty of the painting touched him, and also that he was a man who liked his mother. She had always trusted men who cared for their mothers. They tended to treat women with dignity rather than suspicion.

Conversation flitted from Lexi's interest in art, to his roots in San Francisco, to his recent transfer from London. Both thought Boston had merit. It was easy to agree on food for dinner. Both wanted sushi and there was a good Japanese restaurant in Lexi's neighborhood. As they walked, she admired the easy way he carried himself.

Once there, with Lexi's approval, David ordered two large sakis. She noted his mastery of Japanese etiquette as he filled her cup from her container, put it back on the table, then paused. Lexi, pleased she knew the dance, lifted his saki and poured.

David fixed his eyes as firmly on hers as he'd put his hands on her saki cup, then took his first sip. She followed, and was only out of sync by a second. A bit more uncomfortable with his deep look than she might have imagined, Lexi was the first to break contact, and reached for the menu. David kept up the conversation, smoothing any lingering awkwardness.

It had been years since Lexi had gone on a blind date, but Shakti had been right to put them together. Both Shakti and David had been working at Adler, LaSalle and Thomas for fifteen years, but Shakti had just gotten to know him when he joined the Boston office.

David continued to guide the conversation, and talked engagingly about an internship he'd done at a Tokyo architecture firm after his first year studying at M.I.T. The mere mention of Asia triggered thoughts of Zheng, and Lexi's mind drifted to images of the tenderness they'd shared. Zheng had put her in touch with her needs. Lexi was open to the next possibility and ripe for something that had the potential to last. David seemed so accessible and grounded. Lexi felt safe with him.

Happy to talk about Asia, Lexi knew less about Japan, and said her relationship with the culture was more visual. Years ago a business trip had taken her there. She'd inhaled the Oriental touch in everything from clothing to gardens, dance, and the theater. It was the ritualistic approach to social interaction that Lexi found most unusual.

She described stumbling across a park district recreation center one afternoon in Kyoto, and how it was a powerful glimpse of the disciplined way young boys and girls approached kendo, a physical and mental exercise. The training was clearly passionate, but seemed a bit regimented. The controlled movements of bodies had been a bit frightening in their intensity, but overall the exercise had dimensions of spirituality that Lexi often thought about when she needed to find a quiet place inside her soul.

"The paradox of the chrysanthemum and the sword," she said, still somewhat overwhelmed. "The whole culture seems to glide between beauty and the threat of violence."

"Yes, I saw that, too. I prefer living here." Shifting his body, he kept the conversation moving. "Tell me about your work."

"I develop strategies to double, triple and quadruple the revenue of communication companies we acquire, and I work with operations people to make it happen. We're experimenting with some satellite television programming for a venture in Asia," Lexi said.

"What's included?"

"Movies. Sports. Some reruns. There's original programming for young kids, though."

"What do you like?"

"Well, I'm a soft touch for TV dramas. And I'm not alone. All over the world, evening soaps. There seems to be a steady market for other people's anxiety at the end of the day."

There was a small pocket of silence.

"What's on your mind these days?" Lexi asked.

"Business is good. There's a lot of growth, as I'm sure Shakti has mentioned. But I've been preoccupied by my kid brother."

"Ah, family."

"It's a bad habit. Left over from childhood, I suppose."

"Family?" Lexi said, teasing.

"Patterns. And he's just three years younger. On the small side, but scrappy. And, somehow, I've always protected him."

"Like a bodyguard."

"It started when he was ten. Some bullies stole his bike, and I stepped in."

"My mother once beat up some kids who were picking on her brother."

"Believe me, I wasn't brave, just cagey. I used to carry around a deck of cards, and had a hunch I could coax these guys into a game. Sort of macho. Anyway, I bet them one hundred dollars for the bike and won."

"I didn't know I was dining with a shark," she said, wondering if this was proof of a lotus heart.

"Used to be. And a chain smoker, if you want to know the worst of it. Anyhow, I learned my lesson in Vegas, working on a hotel project. I played blackjack then, and got whipped in a five-deck game."

"You're a card counter?"

"Yeah—but not good enough. Seemed like a good use for quantitative skills."

"So, what's going on now?" she asked, more intrigued than before.

"Johnny's thirty, married, and has a kid. Great time to get over your head in the stock market, huh? Saved him once a couple of years ago, but I don't think it's wise to step in now."

"But you feel you should."

"Those patterns."

"If he saves himself, he might trust himself more."

"Exactly. That's my dilemma." David took the hand on the table and cupped it on top of hers. "How are you doing?"

"Just fine," she said appreciatively. That tender moment was a watershed for the evening. After that, they told more stories, laughed, flirted, and teased each other. Lexi felt no compunction about placing her arm around his waist on the walk home.

She woke up early with thoughts of David. It was just five o'clock, and her mind was racing with images of him and their conversations last night.

Mostly she thought about how much fun they'd had. But don't get too carried away, another voice said. Her grown-up voice. The one she hated to listen to, but was always right when it came to men.

Heading into work ahead of schedule, Lexi's heart quickened when she saw a pink message slip on her desk. At 8:10 A.M. David Morgan had called. Scanning the slip, Lexi confirmed that it was today's date, and that she was supposed to return the call.

Lexi's fervor was flattened when he told her he'd be leaving on Friday for Indonesia.

"I didn't want to bring this up last night," he said softly. "I had no idea how much this would irk me. But I'll be back in two weeks, though suddenly that seems like ages from now. We'll get together immediately." He paused, suddenly seeming a bit shy. "That is, if you'd like to."

"Sure," she said with a sinking feeling. But she remembered everything he said, and replayed the sound of his caring voice all morning, trying to drown out the fear that the separation might dampen his interest in her.

David phoned as soon as he got to Jakarta. The calls came frequently after that. Despite the twelve-hour time change, their random conversations, and the eerie satellite connection, Lexi kept up her spirits.

Mostly, their conversations did a good job of bridging the separation. But just four days before she expected David to return, he phoned to tell her that they'd run into a glitch on the medical center project. The next step for him, as the principal architect, was to stop in Hong Kong to make a presentation to an investment consortium. She heard the echo of her own crushed excitement in his tones. Ironically, that comforted her. He was growing as attached to her as she was to him.

The day after his return, Lexi agreed to meet David at his apartment for drinks before dinner. Understanding the weight of his jet lag, she was happy to save him a trip to pick her up in Brookline. Buoyed by memories of the intimacy of those patch-work, across-the-world conversations, Lexi was attracted to David on a subtle level. Perhaps the long-distance dating had caused them to come closer faster than if they'd been accessible to each other.

Now he was back home. When Lexi arrived at his condo-minium, she was amused to see so many high-rise buildings along the waterfront, close to the historic Faneuil Hall.

With this kaleidoscope of phallic images as her guide, she boarded the elevator in David's building and rode to the thirty-ninth floor. As she stepped out into an intimate hallway adorned with thick wood panels and etched smoked glass, her heart pounded when she saw David waiting outside his apartment.

When he grabbed and hugged her, she was ebullient. Still, the heavy wooden oversized door to his place suggested a style possibly at odds with her own.

She entered the apartment, and felt buoyant as her eyes danced over its creamy walls and carpet. Greeted by a bipanel Oriental screen on the facing wall, she was struck by the deli-cate beauty atop the slick gold paper, bound within a powerful black lacquer frame. It made her shiver.

David moved slowly behind her, as though calibrating the strength of the impulses running though her body. At the end of the hallway, she entered the living room. Black glass encased an otherwise warm room with low suede couches, fine wood-working, and assorted Japanese pots and artifacts.

She loved the contrasts as well as the simplicity and beauty of the lines. Something powerful pulled at her, and as she moved toward the south window, she saw the full moon, separating the sky from the darker ribbon of the Boston Harbor below it. Lexi's body tingled with familiar sensations. Was it intuition or something else?

"What a spectacular place!" she said as she turned to him.

David's eyes shone with the warmth she now found so reassuring. "Quite like it myself," he said, smiling broadly.

Lexi looked at David's face with fascination, recalling the tenderness of their telephone conversations. As he spoke, his lips reminded her of a sunrise starting to take shape. Slipping an arm around her waist, David pressed his lips fully and forcefully on hers. Feeling his ample lips against her mouth, Lexi knew she was with someone whose passion matched her own. As she closed her eyes, she could envision his. What he felt for her had reached the surface, and was reflected on his face. He was warm, sensuous, and deeply knowing.

Deciding on dinner at a neighborhood bistro, they spoke of David's trip. His enthusiasm built as he described the difference the medical center would make in the lives of people throughout Southeast Asia. The state-of-the-art facility was designed as a referral hospital for the most complex medical problems, as well as a first-rate facility for primary care in Jakarta. He won her heart with his goodness and dedication to his work.

Now she was certain he understood more about her as well. Why she was excited about her job, and just how vulnerable, at times, work could make her feel. He clearly relished her descriptions of the communications industry, particularly the tales of hungry venture capitalists ready to wrest the best deals from her hands just when she'd gotten Hockhauser interested in them. But mostly, she sensed that, when he looked at her tonight, he was beginning to see her as the woman she was. Agreeing to go back to his apartment for cognac, she knew she'd be there for the rest of the night.

Stroking her hair as they sat on the sofa, David looked out from the living room at the full moon and said, "I'm charmed by you, Lexi," then paused.

Lexi smiled and played with his collar as she shifted her body closer to his.

"I don't know how many times each day I imagine making love to you. My quantitative skills aren't that good."

Lexi could feel her eyes brighten as she fixed them on his face and said, "Nor are mine."

"Can you stay with me tonight?"

"I'd like that," she said, pressing her thigh against his.

Lexi rose from the couch as David lifted her hand. Lost in the beauty of anticipation, and pleased by how comfortable she felt, Lexi was only faintly aware of her surroundings until they were safe in David's bed. Lifting the remaining flap of Lexi's charmeuse slip, now scrunched around her hips, David's eyes moved above her lower body. Making eye contact again, he, took the edge of the charmeuse between his thumb and forefinger, smiled softly and said, "May I?"

Lexi cast an indelible gaze at the handsome man spread like Poseidon beneath the fanned bottom of a sprightly mermaid. "Yes," she whispered with hardly a breath. And then it began, a symphony of impulses that connected her with this man, and with a deeper power.

Lexi lay back and closed her eyes, reliving the beauty of his face rising between her legs—the bold, rugged features that turned beatific by the light in his eyes and the warmth of his mouth. His quiet charisma was potent as he shared a heartfelt message. Yes, she believed that with David, it all came from the heart. His velvet voice and gentle eyes were merely tools to bring his spirit from the depths.

Allowing herself to be lulled by his magnetism, she relaxed and took all of his pleasure, as her body supplied rich, wet pathways for him to travel. Amused by how quickly she responded, Lexi thought of her labia as a child's backyard slip and slide, and then as the route to her soul. He massaged her flesh as though he was playing a piano concerto, and she wanted more.

David took her clitoris in his mouth, sucking feverishly like a bird finding its favorite food after a long, winter break. Lexi relaxed, believing anything was possible. She could feel her labia swell as they unfolded, like a lily opening to a warming spring. Fed naturally by deep, moist soil, her petals would soon dance like poppies. Mirroring the first movement of a concerto, he added his fingers to the mix. She let him stretch out each lip with light, airy strokes and with the rhythm, her skin thickened.

Lexi gloried in the long, slow strokes of the piano concerto's second movement as though she could hear the music in her ears and wriggled to meet each finger as they roamed her orifices. With the patience of a rosebud, she basked in the heat. Opening herself up to him with the grace of a long-stemmed American Beauty, her clitoris hardened.

The rebirth at hand, Lexi seethed as David tapped rapidly on her clitoris in the final movement of his concerto. In a fevered pitch, she gave way. She was free and felt as beautiful as an orchid, petals opening.

Turning to change positions, Lexi started to edge down the sheets when David pulled at her arm. "Stay close so I can touch you," he said.

Arched forward from a seated position, David kneaded her buttocks as she, at his side, draped herself over his cock. Then he stroked her long, blonde curls with the firm touch of a sculptor, able to release the spirit within her as she took him into her mouth.

Sparked by his warm caresses, Lexi had an urge to make everything happen at once. Working with both lips and both hands, she fell into a delirious tempo. Licking. Sucking. Squeezing.

"Whoa," he said with a laugh.

Gripping her shoulder, David slid to the side and in one motion pulled Lexi's hips to the edge of the bed as he stood, towering over the king-size mattress. Lexi stayed loose to follow his lead, her legs wrapped lightly around his waist. She wished she were as light as a teenager, then lost the thought as he slipped a pillow under her bottom, and thrust his cock deep inside. Her earthiness took hold. Lexi's heart swirled and with legs laced behind his waist, she felt her lust simmer. Screaming out when he pressed her legs back like a jackknife, Lexi's heels snapped over his shoulders.

Still clutching her hips, David thrust himself faster and deeper into her loamy soil, and lost control. Pushing her back further on the bed, he moved forward on his knees. No longer tracking, Lexi yelled when, like a hot iron, he flattened her out with his burning, hard body. On fire, she split open.

Saturday night became Sunday and then early Monday morning. When Lexi left David's apartment, she soaked up the markers of spring with all of her senses. The air, still dense with moisture from last night's rain, mixed up the smells of spring like an assortment of blossoms in a bride's bouquet. Three white amelanchiers flanked the entryway of a favorite Beaux Art building. The spray of white light from the network of taut branches in full boom lifted Lexi's soul.

The background song of the birds had a quieting effect. Lexi turned the corner and her eyes lit on something behind the elegant wrought-iron fence of a stately stone mansion. There, on a green rubberized tarp that covered a grouping of furniture not yet ready for summer use, a sparrow was celebrating dawn.

Nestled in a large fold of the tarp, the bird was surrounded by fresh rainwater. Rhythmically dropping his head, he took small sips, creating concentric circles in the water around him. Bobbing, he toasted the beauty of spring.

Stopping home quickly to change clothes, she made it to work by eight o'clock. Moments later, David called. "Hey, gorgeous," he said. "I'm thinking about heading over and carrying you out of that posh office of yours. How about France? Or anywhere?"

"I'd love it," Lexi said. Hockhauser would give her the time off. That or she would take it, and go without a backward glance. Love was within her reach. Nothing else was more important right now.

"Seriously. It's been too long since I've taken any time for myself. How about you?"

"Really?"

"Absolutely. Whatever you want."

"I could spend every vacation in France."

"How did I know?" he said.

"Have you been to Mont Saint Michel?" Lexi asked.

"In Normandy? No. Just Rouen and the D-day beaches."

"Great—let's do it," Lexi cried, then steadied herself. "If that's okay. With you, I mean . . ."

"No need to be tentative, Alexis Lankford. I'd say we're beyond that, wouldn't you?"

A week later when they landed at Charles de Gaulle, Lexi was still tingling. David had planned the trip, and merely asked her to bless the itinerary. They were driving from Paris on the highway, and then would take some of the scenic routes, stopping off along the way. The trick was to arrive at Mont Saint Michel at low tide. Rich images of the granite island swept away the last bit of gravity that kept Lexi hovering just above the earth.

Right now, the highway supplied its own thrill. Cars of all makes and sizes whizzed along the forest-lined passage at a steady ninety to 110 miles per hour, and the danger was palpable. Though she hardly considered herself risk averse, the cars hurtling around them reminded her that the French were descended from the Gauls—a nation whose soldiers waged war naked. David seemed happy to zip along with the rushing traffic, so she let go of her fear and let him take charge.

Soon they were at Le Pin Stud, France's famous horse-breeding center. Lexi had made a special point of including it in the itinerary. She'd had an odd affinity to horses since childhood, and the sight of the Norman thoroughbred at the gate pulled at her soul: the sensuous lines of its spine, the mirror image of its belly, the graceful face.

Arms around each other's backs, Lexi and David strolled around the grounds. The hot walkers were friendly and invited them to stay while they worked out the racehorses. The two of them mostly watched the trainers take the thoroughbreds over a series of jumps constructed by an architect known for the difficult courses he'd designed all over the world. Rider and horse became one. Each jump required an equal measure of grace and power. Lexi, attuned to the rhythm of the horses' rise and fall, wanted to soar with them.

They wandered awhile until Lexi had an odd feeling, possibly a premonition, and felt the urge to get to Mont Saint Michel. The need to move forward overpowered her. They lost themselves in the Auge countryside. Twisting through Vallée

d'Enfer, Lexi savored the mix of trees under the dense interlocking canopy of oaks, beeches, and firs. The beauty of this
place, known as Hell Valley, was daunting. A stream, a thousand
feet below, snaked through the primeval forest. She understood
in that moment the crazy logic that might tempt a person who
was broken-hearted to plummet to her death in pursuit of sweet
oblivion.

She grew calmer as they passed through small villages where
each stone farmhouse had a small orchard. Amid the blossom-
ing trees were cows with beatific eyes and barrel-shaped
bodies—miles and miles of Norman cows, strung together like
ornaments across front lawns in every village. Watching the
cows calmed her. The animals' peaceful way of doing nothing
showed her something new: how to be.

"I feel more like myself right now than I have in years," she
said. They had not exchanged more than a dozen words since
leaving the stud farm.

"You look so happy."

"And you?" she asked, jerking her head slightly, afraid the day
might not mean as much to him.

"I don't know when I've ever enjoyed myself more."

Her first view of Mont Saint Michel raced like electric current through her serenity. From a distance, it seemed ethereal
against the gray-blue sea that lashed at its granite base. The
solitude was haunting. Majestic and commanding, the church
rose from the sea, claiming its space on the planet. The beauty
spoke to all parts of her. Still eight miles away, she'd merged in
an instant with thousands of years of Mont Saint Michel's
sacred mythology. Connecting with something so momentous
buoyed her spirits. Anything was possible if this magical island
existed—even love and peace.

Lexi felt teary, then noticed she'd been holding her breath.

David must have noticed the effect the island had on her. He'd stopped the car at the side of the road, and when he put his hand on hers, she felt grounded again.

"It's magnificent, isn't it?" he said. David turned and looked quizzically at her, as if wondering how he could help guide her fantasy.

"Let's get out of the car," she said softly.

The air was crisp and the wind picked up, moving the clouds overhead so quickly that the mottled light no more than dotted their bodies before passing by. Lexi reached her arm around David's waist and nosed her head into his shoulder. She felt about the mountain like a young woman slowly readying herself to meet a new lover for the second time—wondering if everything would be just as good as the first time. How had she fallen in love with this spot she'd never visited before? Was it the dreamy pictures she had often seen in travel magazines?

They drove the rest of the way in near silence, parking the car at the edge of the sandy beach, now the only physical barrier between them and the island shrine. Arriving like a medieval pilgrim, Lexi gave herself to the experience. She emptied her mind of any thought and surrendered to the moment.

Her footprints sank into the wet sand slowly, in sync with the pace of the sun's descent. Hand-in-hand, she and David crossed a stretch of beach that at low tide could span twelve miles. Heading in from a narrower point, they had less than a mile to go. Most of the day's tourists had already gone, on their way to nearby towns to dine on Norman specialties. She was grateful that they'd arrived late in the day, guaranteeing them privacy.

When Lexi turned to give David a smile, he pulled at her hand, bringing them to a stop. With the wind at his back, the shadow of his body lay at an angle on the wet sand. He took

Lexi in his arms and kissed her, first forcefully, then tenderly working his tongue into her mouth.

Mont Saint Michel was conceived in the eleventh century when St. Michael appeared to a local abbot, asking that a church be built on France's most dangerous coast. Lexi could imagine the zeal with which the pilgrims hauled granite from the Chausey Islands to the top of the rock, 250 feet above a raging sea. Galvanized by the dream and the mission, they earned St. Michael's protection along this deadly stretch. The commitment was what made the difference. Lexi wondered if what she felt for David was a love so pure that she could pursue it— against all odds—with the same fevered passion.

Within five minutes, they were at the door of La Mere Poulard, a charming inn with only twelve rooms. Arrangements were made to have their bags brought up from the car. Dinner was set for seven-thirty. Lexi gazed lovingly at the slanted ceiling of their tiny room, which overlooked the bay. One lone chair, delicately carved, was placed close to a green fringed lampshade that emitted just enough light for a seance. Cut-glass wall sconces evened out the glow. Lexi was charmed by their secret hideaway.

Washing down the spring lamb with wine, then coffee and a shot of Calvados, Normandy's apple liquor, Lexi was experiencing a new aspect of herself. Her inner life finally seemed merged with her life on the physical plane. Detached from everything but her happiness, she glanced over the candles at David, and ran her tongue slowly along her well-fed lips. He smiled and took the cue.

Back in their room, Lexi knew their lovemaking would be different against this backdrop. The big unknown was just how deep, or high, she'd let herself go tonight. David had learned to unlock her feelings, and she felt blessed. She changed quickly into a short chiffon nightshirt and nestled under the feather comforter.

Laughing out loud, she called across the room to David, who was just returning from the bathroom. "Bedsprings! Can you believe it? We have bedsprings!"

"If it's good enough for pilgrims, it's good enough for me," he yelled back. Then he pounced on top of her. They wrestled as the metal twisted and turned beneath them.

"A temptress like you is no match for an indomitable archangel," David said when she pinned him on his back.

"I'm more dangerous than you think," she said, rising above him and running her hand along his loins.

"Prove it," he taunted, as relaxed as a Norman cow.

Much as she liked to switch things around and take charge of the lovemaking from time to time, tonight the ploy had greater import. For Lexi, the only real question when she and David made love was whether they'd reach that rare point of transcendence. Increasingly, she understood that such wonder had to do with them both being open to a powerful exchange on the same night. Sitting between David's widespread legs, she motioned him to slide back against the headboard. She stretched her legs out under his bent knees, and rested them on either side of his body.

"First, I need to hypnotize you," she said, nearly in her own trance.

"You already have, babe," he said, slowly moving his head from side to side.

"Just look at me and we'll breathe together."

Lexi let her eyes soften to the melting point. She was ready to take his emotions anywhere he'd let them go, and she was far enough away to see David's chest expand as he slowly inhaled the sea air. With bedroom eyes, she guided him in a string of repetitions, breathing in and out together.

Within moments, she felt glued to his body in an erotic exchange of electrical impulses. She watched David's eyes flicker as he did the same. Lexi felt her eyes brighten, then David's mouth widened to a smile. Tilting her head to the side, she savored his gentle face and recognized the spark. In a split second, their encounter changed. The world receded and Lexi could no longer feel the air on her back. They were transformed. Like one organism, they'd come together and were bound by spirit.

David gently reached forward and pressed back on Lexi's belly. She laid down, edging her feet up toward the headboard and tucked them behind David's backside. From the warmth of his eyes, she knew there was no reason to hurry tonight—that he'd let her take as much time as she wanted. She stretched back and took everything he wanted to give as her pelvis rocked gently under the pressure of his fingers.

Wondering if he felt the ridges of that wondrous circle of skin inside her pelvis swell, before or at about the same time she went under his spell, she let go of the thought and felt blessed that he, too, knew some magic. Panting to coax the cooling salt air down her lungs, Lexi floated through the long stretch of orgasms. The ecstasy triggered images of so many other enchanted nights with David. Washed by the memories, her spirits soared. The rapture took her deep inside, springing loose a rush of primal growls.

Lifting herself up and reaching over to David, she was taken aback when he shook his head as she reached for his hard cock. That's when David moved to his knees and raised himself above her. The shadow of his shoulders stretched from one side to the other of their narrow room. As his chest rose, so did his rippled muscles. When he drew in his next breath, Lexi imagined that he was the size and shape of St. Michael. So powerful and majestic, he entered her in one fluid motion. And with her head at the foot of the bed, alongside his, she rode him with the speed of the high tide at a full moon, like a horse galloping toward Mont Saint Michel.

Lexi could only see a red blur through her closed eyes. The color washed her eyeballs like sea spray. Some moments it was streaky and faint, then suddenly it pulsed like a beacon. In time, she lost track of everything but the blaze. Her hands, chest, and face were on fire, until suddenly the fever broke. She felt filled with something stranger than helium, floating upward, as though to be swallowed by the heavens.

They'd brought each other to paradise more than once, so beautiful and different each time. Euphoric, she quivered and shook. She might just as well have been one of the waves that rode twelve miles to butt up against Mont Saint Michel's base. She felt powerful and calm, confident that the ride was never ending.

Unconscious of how she was restraining her sounds in the tiny room with paper-thin walls, she felt the pressure mount. Behind her eyes flashed an ox-blood red, followed by white light that shot through her lenses and up to her forehead. Lexi was tucked within a brilliant cocoon. She had everything she'd ever wanted in life, and tears of joy streamed down her face.

As she closed her eyes, David whispered, "*Magnifique.*"

"*D'accord,*" she purred.

Lexi fell asleep with her body wound around David's.

When she awoke, he was already in the shower and she stretched her feet toward the window, wondering if she'd be too late to suds his tight butt. Pulling off the covers, she hurried to the bathroom and flung open the glass door. Eyes closed, with water running down his face, he stayed still, except for a slight smile.

"Looks like you're thinking about the Bayeux Tapestry, that legend of Norman bravery," she said enthusiastically.

"Exactly," he said with a smirk.

When he pulled her close to him, she twisted out of his arms. "I have to be more careful than that. It's pornographic stuff, you know."

"Sounds like I'm going to have to agree to something if I want to know what's going on."

"I've always wanted to see the Bayeux Tapestry. My mother does all kinds of needlework. Crewel embroidery. Complicated knitting. Crocheting. And once she showed me a picture of the tapestry. Told me needlework was God's way of keeping women out of trouble. She said they must have had a competition to see who'd get to embroider the man with the penis the length of his thigh."

"What? On the tapestry?"

"You bet. You don't think that all those ancient women's craft gatherings were only about sewing, do you?"

"I never want to stop seeing the world through your eyes, babe."

"Maybe you won't have to," Lexi said with a wink.

This time Lexi took the wheel. On the road to Bayeux she told David everything she knew about Queen Matilda's tapestry, which was actually a piece of embroidery. As they walked into the museum, she was struck by what a gift her mother had given her by talking about it. Mamma must have memorized every embroidered inch on the 230 feet of the linen tapestry, five panels wide. She'd probably be able to recreate freehand most of the action on the tableau with her well tutored hands—the fine wool stitchwork of the ships, soldiers, and livestock. Men with hacked-off heads, one with an arrow through his eye. Lexi imagined her mother rubbing and circling back over the crosshatches, resurrecting this masterpiece from the Middle Ages, figuring out the story it told, with no need of a handbook or guide.

When they got to the end of the tableau, David gave her a squeeze and said, "It's remarkable."

"Yep. Pure female magic."

Dinner was another serene interlude. Everything was coming together for Lexi on this trip. Normandy touched her in ways that other beautiful spots never had.

The country was blessed with every type of natural beauty imaginable. Long stretches of sandy beach merged with rocky caves and wide open bays. Enormous sand dunes leveled off and met up with green valleys and lush pastures, home to the six million head of cattle in the region.

Lexi spread the creamy Pont l'Eveque cheese on her bread, imagining it was poured from milk still warm from the cow. Cheese as an aphrodisiac. She ran her tongue around her mouth again as she took David's hand, heading back to the room in a dreamy mood.

Lexi sensed something when David opened the door. He moved quickly into the room, then stopped, holding her arms just above the elbow.

"Lexi, I'm in love with you and always will be. There are few things in life that have ever been so clear. I feel it when we're together and I feel it when we're apart. Twelve weeks, and I know you are the love of my life."

"Oh, David," Lexi sighed. "I feel the same. Especially when I first wake up in the morning. I'm so happy, I feel like I can fly."

"Don't try," he said, as he squeezed her.

"If I do, I'll take you along," she said lightly.

With his head tilted down, he stretched his neck toward her and said, "Lexi, will you marry me"?

"I might have asked you first, you know," she said softly. "Yes, David. I will." Then her emotion broke, "I'm so happy, David. And scared."

"Me, too," he said, enfolding her in his arms.

Tenderly, she whispered, "I'll give you my best, lover. And make you a little crazy sometimes."

"That's the fine print," he said.

"Yes, and there's more."

"I'm listening," he said, as the light from the moon outside the window danced with the light in his eyes.

"Do you promise to keep that spark in your eyes?"

"You bet."

"And, will you tell me when you think I'm nuts?"

"That's easy," he said with a ready laugh. "And you? Will you scrunch your nose up and make faces at me, even when we're old?"

Pursing her lips, Lexi thought about it for a moment and said, "If I have to."

"And," he said, as his voice cracked a bit, "keep touching me the way you do, Lexi, with your whole being."

Lexi let out something between a gasp and a squeal. Reaching toward David's face, she smoothed his temple with her palm. Their lips met with even pressure. It was as though a higher force had taken charge and worked quickly, like an artist with a paintbrush. Lexi imagined that bound together, they were like the yin-yang symbol, black and white, neatly separated by a gentle curve. A master teacher, moving the paintbrush back and forth, blurred the boundaries as their bodies merged with the same mysterious speed.

Just before she fell asleep, Lexi whispered, "Forevermore," to herself as she visualized the two of them soaring in a tiny wicker basket tied to a gold spun, hot air balloon.

In the morning, she awoke first. Still awed by what happened last night, Lexi needed some space to put it all together. She crept out of bed and groped for a pair of cotton leggings and a T-shirt, hoping to sneak out before David woke up.

Once in the hallway, she took a deep breath, then headed toward the beach, stopping at the desk to leave her huge key, a metal replica of Mont Saint Michel fastened by a silk tassel. Climbing down the steps, she felt freer, but something was still racing beneath the surface.

When she got to the beach, she loosened up. The beauty reassured her, and she was less queasy. Her lungs felt as expansive as the sky.

She walked along the water, looking up at the salt marshes, then back at Mont Saint Michel, and headed to the point past the marshes, conjuring up images of her lovemaking with David. It felt like a pilgrimage, possibly her first. What happened, although she hadn't realized it at the time, was that she'd connected to something sacred. "My God," she cried in disbelief. It was like something Shakti once described—the pilgrim's journey within the sacred mountain.

Shakti had been making pilgrimages to temples in India with her family since her teens. She said the first ones were a turning point. That's when she'd started to feel the sacred in her body. Even now, Shakti said, the same images helped her connect to the divine.

Lexi visualized the images of India that Shakti once described. The pilgrims, miles and miles of them, walking a steady pace to the sacred cave at Elephanta. Lexi's body must have cried out, as theirs did, for something more before it happened. What was it? Perhaps a sense of completeness, so hard to find in all but a few places. Maybe that's what she'd found with David, and this morning it took her breath away.

What kinds of stories lured so many Indian pilgrims to the mountain temple? She knew they came in droves and returned as often as possible, with the single purpose of moving deep within a mountain. Imagining how they felt groping their way along the low-lit passageway into the mountain, she wondered when they could first see the glow of the warm interiors.

Did their searching eyes race along the delicate carvings of dancing female bodies on the stone walls? Did the ritual bathe their senses? Walking, as if in a meditation, they quieted the mind and opened the heart. And once deep inside, each pilgrim was rewarded. Each was wedded to the moment.

But how could the journey ever meet their expectations? What could consummate the lengthy search for something invisible? For every traveler, it was the same. The transformation happened in the last room—the most sacred part of the temple. Lexi imagined entering the room, shaped like a vulva, with its sinewy borders. In the center was a stone lingam. First titillated, then scared by the mystery, she grew accustomed to being in the presence of these ancient female and male symbols. The intimacy centered her. She felt giddy. The journey was complete. Sexuality and spirituality were one. For each it was the same.

Yes, Lexi realized, that's exactly what had happened with David. Maybe that's why David asked her to marry him. Was that why she'd said yes so quickly, and with such certainty? Was he just as surprised this morning? Could they recreate those sensations over a lifetime? With so many other natural bonds, she believed they would.

Now it all made perfect sense to her. The feelings swirled around her belly as she watched the water swish back and forth around Mont Saint Michel at mid-tide. How long could *they* stay at mid-tide—that uncanny point of balance?

Lexi turned and raced to the hotel. She wanted to throw her arms around him and shout with glee. He was hers now. Forever and ever. She picked up speed.

SUMMER

One is not born a woman, one becomes one.

~ SIMONE DE BEAUVOIR

"Hey, Tiger," Lexi said, giving Rob, her eight-year-old, a big hug as he came through the screen door. "How was your day?"

"Okay," he said with little emotion.

"Is the camp cool?" she asked.

"Yeah, it's all right," he said, opening the refrigerator door. He pulled last night's leftover pasta from the lower shelf, followed by the jar of sauce.

"All right?" she asked, lifting a bowl for him from the cupboard.

"It's just that the kids are different. Sort of annoying," he said, spooning pasta into the bowl.

"You mean, there are some you don't like?" she said, getting him a fork from the drawer.

"Yeah. I guess," he said, as he topped the heaping pile of spiral rotini with red sauce.

"What's the yuckiest one like?" she asked, catching his eye.

"He looks like me, but he's a lot bigger," he said, turning to face her before putting his bowl in the microwave.

"And that's bad?" she asked, running her hand along the side of her hair.

"It was when he hit me," he said, punching the microwave buttons hard.

"Hit you?" she repeated in even tones.

"Some kids were teasing him. He lives near the airport in Winthrop. They said a plane could crash on him," Rob explained, putting the half-full Plexiglas container back in the part of the refrigerator they called the pasta pit.

"So, he hit you?"

"I was standing near those kids."

"Then what?"

"I tried to talk to him instead of hitting back. Just like you said."

"And?"

"He told me to shut up. Then he hit me again."

"Rob," Lexi said slowly, but firmly. "He hit you once. And then he hit you a second time. Sweetie, if he hits you again, he'll always hit you."

"Are you saying I should hit him back?" Rob asked with alarm.

"Yes. You have to. He's a bully," Lexi said.

Rob's return look was unreadable. The microwave pinged, giving Lexi a chance to think as her son got busy with the pasta. God, it was hard to have to teach him that life was not always fair.

She didn't know why the incident should surprise her. Young boys were bound to stake out their turf on the first day of camp. She would prefer better supervision, but knew that boys are programmed to set up a pecking order. When no one's looking, some will push the boundaries. Lexi also had enough experience with Rob's coaches to know that most would tolerate a fair amount of rough play.

She joined him at the bistro table while he wolfed down his pasta. Lexi thought back to the days when it was easy to protect him. How she'd loved holding his sturdy, two-year-old body, and waited for the moment each evening when he would give up the breakneck speed of his day and dissolve in her arms. The older he got, the tighter he held onto the frenetic pace. Sometimes, though, after a bath, he'd sit in her lap for a story, one they either read or made up together. Lexi could sense the moment he'd sink toward her bosom, then rest like the babe she'd nursed at her breast for over a year and a half.

Lexi felt blessed to have a son. "If it happens" is what she'd always said. It would be great if it happened. She and David had both wanted a child.

But pregnancy didn't "just happen." A month after they were married, Lexi made an appointment to see her gynecologist, and was surprised when he showed her numbers suggesting that at her age, she'd have to do more than wait to conceive. Getting pregnant was not a sure thing.

"At thirty-four, it could take quite a while," Dr. Gallanis said. "I'm not trying to discourage you. I just want you to know the facts."

Facts, then colored bar charts, plus paraphernalia. Lexi left the office clutching a blank form in her sweaty palm. She was to record the critical data—lovemaking. With visions of thermometers, standard and electronic, to tell her when but not how, Lexi headed to the drugstore. In the narrow aisles, she found kits to pinpoint ovulation. But how to isolate her fertile moments was not the end of it. There was more to do. Pay attention to diet, exercise, and stress levels. And if she believed

Shakti, her thought patterns. If she really wanted a child, she'd conceive. Within a year, they were three. Lexi stopped working two weeks before the baby was due, and never regretted her decision to recast her professional life to stay close to Rob.

But he needed her less now, at least her constant presence. As if to prove it, he finished his snack and immediately moved onto the next activity.

"Jerry's dad put up a skateboard ramp for us. I'll see you later."

"Be safe," she started to say, then caught herself. Recently David had pointed out to her that she was spending too much energy worrying about Rob. Sighing, Lexi reflexively began to clean Rob's place, only to realize he had already cleaned up after himself.

In just a few days, David's mother would be visiting for a long weekend, and Lexi still had some items on her to-do list for Mom's visit. Checking her lipstick in the mirror, she opted to remain dressed in the black cotton leggings and long T-shirt from her morning workout to do her shopping.

An hour or so later, she returned to the gracious home she and David had bought soon after Rob was born. Chestnut Hill was just outside of Boston, and boasted some of the best schools in the state. The sleek, beige masonry of her Italian villa was beautifully proportioned on five acres of land. It was as magnificent as the Roman compounds Lexi loved to read about in middle school, with their progression of rooms, courtyards and colonnades. Lexi's life was one she only dared imagine as a young girl.

Every time Lexi pulled into the double-entry driveway, she pinched herself when she caught sight of the elegant wrought iron gate that gracefully gave way to the clean simplicity of the architecture.

As Lexi edged her way into the garage, she tried to stop just short of the tennis ball David had suspended from the ceiling to slow her speedier returns. A way to protect both her fender and the wall. Pressing hard on the brakes, she felt a thud just as the ball hit the windshield. The yellow fuzz of the florescent, marigold colored ball reminded her of so many other parts of her day. She wondered if there were too many controls in a life that once knew no bounds.

As she pressed her Jaguar forward, she dredged up uncomfortable images of David's detachment. The way he kept his arms crossed over his chest when they talked. How he'd dismiss things she or Rob said, shaking his head rather than listening, always seeming miles away. A heavier travel load and more challenges at the firm had made it a tiring year for him—and for Lexi.

Lexi remembered how before the wedding nine years ago he'd promised to travel less. They'd spent a number of charmed years before he slipped back into his old ways.

Sliding the packages slowly toward her from the backseat, Lexi headed into the food pantry, through the side door and the mud room. Pleased that she'd thought to pick up some crusty bread to serve with the prosciutto and melon, she was back in time to arrange the flowers that she'd cut that morning, just after sunrise.

Once in the kitchen, Lexi felt grounded. From the window over the sink, she could see a portion of the garden. The summer colors were spectacular. Had she ever had more flowers or more variety than this year? The terrace outside her kitchen window was the first of three levels behind the house.

Cascading down the hillside, the gardens leveled off at a swimming pool at the bottom of the hill. Lexi had cultivated each parcel as though nurturing a new friendship. Just three years ago she'd cradled muddy bulbs in her fertile hands. The results were gifts, miracles.

She had poured her creative juices into designing the garden. Identifying, selecting, and laying in plant material. The tricky part was imagining each season in three dimensions. She'd taken out an old sketchbook and played with colored chalk to get a glimpse. Now the sea grasses wiggled while the astilbe stood erect. The azaleas were as glamorous as Loretta Young. While the rhododendrons were just past their peak, the hydrangeas had a sculpted, soft look. Lexi smiled, knowing that by August, the anemones would have their romp.

Crisscrossing the stalks of the purple irises with bright yellow centers and the candy-cane-colored Rubrum lilies, she had an idea. Why not add the hot orange Gerber daisies she'd already wired to the dinner centerpiece? Inspired by their playful beauty, Lexi wedged the stems between the clear marbles at the base of the deep, crystal bowl. Back and forth, her hands set a fluid pace, much like braiding hair. Startled by the memory of her hair being plaited so skillfully in Barbados, years ago, she reached for a purplish peony to punctuate the moment. Her fantasy shifted when she heard David come through the door, much earlier than usual. Lexi moved quickly to greet him.

"Hi, sweetheart," he said. She flung her arms around him and felt a release as she pressed her pelvis to his. David held her longer than usual, and slowly moved his hands around her back, then rested them on her buttocks.

Giving her a big squeeze, he said, "How about a swim?" The proposition conjured up all the romantic interludes in their marriage that involved beaches, lakes, and oceans, as well as their own backyard pool.

"You bet," she said and slowly moved her lips seductively.

Running his hand down her bottom, he goosed her lightly.

"Beat you there," she called as she made a fast break and took the stairs two at a time.

Lexi pulled a black suit with a long slit down the center from one of the wide, shallow drawers of her built-in cabinet. Brass rectangles joined the two sides of the daring top. She shifted her breasts so her cleavage was shown to the best advantage. She wondered what her role model, O'Keeffe, might have thought about boob lifts. That was always enough to dissuade her when a look in the mirror let her see the difference between twenty-six and forty-two.

Satisfied with the suit's sultry fit, she straightened her shoulders, and took a quick look at herself in the closet mirror. She liked what she saw. The way her bosom overflowed the small cups linked together by gold metal, embossed with the ancient Chinese key pattern. Studying the symbol for a moment she smiled, then sighed. Her eyes rested on her rounded stomach. The suit's long slit came to a close just above her waist, and she forgave herself the soft mound. She was conscious of the earthy swell of her pelvis and she laughed out loud when she checked to see if it showed up in the mirror.

Sensing she might still be in the lead, Lexi streamed out of her dressing room and pulled a towel from the linen closet as she raced down the hallway. Feeling David at her heels, she beat him down the stairs and tucked into the stairwell. In wait, she rolled up her towel and swatted him as he passed her by.

"I consider that a declaration of war," he laughed, and grabbed it away. Turning the towel into a belt, he lassoed her and pulled her through the kitchen and out onto the terrace.

Well-trained by watching Rob tussle with his friends, Lexi hung back and made hissing noises until they reached the glass door that opened onto the portico. With the instinct of a samurai warrior, she seized the moment. David paused to slide the door open. Squatting and ducking, all at once, she freed herself and let out an enormous squeal as she bolted down the terrace.

Lexi felt beautiful as she plunged into the pool. As always, swimming smoothed out any rocky emotions. She fanned out her arms and pushed the water away from her body, diving deep. Opening her eyes, she saw the base of the silver ladder on the other side. She headed toward the deep end, hoping to gain another few yards before David could catch her.

But David stopped her, grabbed her ankles, and wrapped his legs tight around her backside. He used her body like a diver's "life line," a vertical rope. Lexi protested as she surfaced, but only slightly. Was it the way David clenched his arms around her back or the tender kiss on her neck? All mixed up, their body parts a jumble, she said surrendering, "I'm yours."

Boosting herself up with her legs around his waist, she pulled his head toward her. Like two dolphins mating with nothing more than big open smiles, they gnawed and nibbled at each other. Delighted to feel David's hands sink down around her pelvis, Lexi reeled when she heard a piercing cry.

"I'm hungry," Rob yelled. He was standing at the foot of the pool.

Tilting her head back, as if to wrest herself from a delicious consciousness, Lexi beamed at Rob, planted so adamantly at the edge of the pool.

"Or should I just dive in, too, Mom?" he asked with glee.

"Sweetheart. You're right. It's time to eat. We'll be right there."

David swam to the steps and jumped out to give Rob a hug. Rob and David talked about the incident at baseball camp, and Rob showed his father a new batting technique. As Lexi watched Rob swing his arms, she fixed on her first image of him. From birth he had been as kinetic as a Chinese puppet and possessed with great spirit. He had wiggled way beyond his snug receiving blanket and stretchy hat on the delivery room table. From the moment of his birth, his eyes shone with wisdom. Time stopped—now as then. Lexi relived the moment.

Happy to see Rob and David pal around together and play ball, Lexi floated for a bit in the pool, lapsing deeper into the memory of Rob's birth. How frightened she'd been to be so big. Yet determined to give birth differently—at least, more organically. From midnight to midmorning, they worked with almond oil, tennis balls, lollipops, and popsicles. They'd made love at home during the early stages of labor. Somewhere during her pregnancy she had gotten the notion that sex during early labor would bring her body in tune with the process of releasing the love inside her. Looking back, it seemed more romantic than practical—ushering the baby out of the womb in the way it was conceived.

Must have been one of Shakti's ideas, Lexi thought to herself, turning over to work on her breaststroke.

Looking up at the canopy of trees, her mind swirled with images of Rob's birth. She'd felt so awful once tethered by the hospital regimen. Not to mention how it slowed her labor. In the birthing room, they weathered a stream of residents, nurses, and the one predelivery visit of Dr. Gallanis. Lexi had fought to keep her faith in soft music and tender words.

Then came the moment when she lost control. The light seeping through the thick clouds overhead softened the jolt she felt just thinking about it. Fully dilated, she gave way to the seismic pressure within. As an orderly rolled her to the delivery room her body rose and fell of its own volition. *"Is everybody ready?"* she remembered yelling out. *"What's going on here? Is everybody here? What are we doing?"*

Lexi almost lost touch with David as the chaos broke, then she felt him again, kneeling at her side. Squeezing hands, they took the last part of the journey together. With nothing stronger than an analgesic to numb the pain, Lexi's pants grew tribal. Even now she bridled as she relived the exhilaration and the raw fear. Surrendering, she mustered energy she had never known before.

"Push. Push," Dr. Gallanis said in low tones that resonated like a drum roll. Tapping into her primitive urges, and clenching David's hand, Lexi was one with David when Rob arrived.

During dinner that night, she was still enmeshed in the memory of Rob's birth. Every word said, the simple conversation between her husband and son was heightened by reminiscing about her labor. Lexi marveled at the strong, confident, young boy Rob had become. And how that thirty-six-hour interlude had birthed this miracle—her child, their family. Happier than she had felt in quite a while, she turned to David. As the candlelight flickered, she saw once more the beauty inside him.

How long would it be, she wondered, before she would have the luxury of another simple night with "her guys?"

She and David went to bed earlier than usual. David seemed less stressed out than he had for more time than she cared to remember. Was it a few weeks? Months? How long ago had it been since they had snuggled under the cotton quilt Lexi had taken from her childhood bedroom in the family's summer-house on the Delaware?

Seizing the moment, she reviewed with him the plans for Grandma Morgan's Fourth of July visit. But before they could finish, his eyes closed, and she stopped talking, and stroked his temples as he drifted off. David would often fight off sleep, wanting that extra half-hour to go over papers for the addition to the medical facility his company was building in Jakarta.

Lexi woke up early the next morning to put the finishing

touches on her mother-in-law's room, including a new full-length mirror and a proper towel bar to replace the hooks in the bathroom. A basket of scented soaps laid out artfully next to the porcelain soap dish she'd brought back from Portugal added a luxurious touch.

Speeding through her checklist, she kept turning over images from moments in the pool before Rob appeared and their lovemaking had been postponed. Lately it was hard to find time. Their lovemaking was sweet, but routine. They needed to get past this plateau. She believed that after nine years of marriage, she and David truly knew how to leave fingerprints on each other's souls.

The weekend plans came off without a hitch. Friday, a light supper. Saturday, dinner at Helen Morgan's favorite restaurant on the Wharf. Sunday, they had tickets for Tchaikovsky's 1812 Overture at Tanglewood.

As they piled into the car, it was obvious that her mother-in-law appreciated the time spent planning the trip. A regal woman, whose impeccable manners reflected the best of her generation, Helen set a high standard for Lexi's family. But today Lexi knew they could be more casual.

Lexi had attended the summer festival in the Berkshires every summer she could remember. Some of her best memories were of coming down from Falmouth on weekends with family and a girlfriend. They did lots of boy watching, snacked constantly, and relished their freedom. As a young adult, for Lexi, Tanglewood had become a place to get tanked up on universal energies and feel the enormity of life. It was a place where Lexi could daydream while being tucked into the bosom of her family.

Lexi led the way into the park, and claimed a spot for their clan. Within minutes the Morgans were happily huddled together on blankets and lawn chairs. With great music and food from a take-out gourmet store, all set against a backdrop worthy of the Impressionists, the concert was an ideal way to give closure to her mother-in-law's visit. They could all feel connected, and recharge at the same time. Once it turned dark, they'd merge with the damp, thick grassy earth and the night sky above.

That's when the feeling shifted. David kept watching the group opposite them. Lexi sensed an uneasiness in David.

Had he spent all the emotion that he had to give to his mother on this visit? Was he, on Sunday evening, locked into the troubles of the week ahead? What was going on? For Lexi, it was all speculation. What was real was what she saw: a drama of seduction.

The three of them faced a covered pavilion where people sat in wooden seats to hear the concert. Out on the grass, they were planted between speakers that would spread the music in all directions. Rob and his friend Elliott tossed a ball at the edge of the park.

A family was seated on blankets just six feet away. The older generation consisted of two middle-aged sisters. Their faces spoke volumes about their struggles, past and present. What Lexi couldn't decipher from the creases on the elder's stern cheeks was obvious enough when she studied the woman's eyes. Opaque and sad, they were a stiff topping for the asymmetrical spine of her tall, thin body.

Lexi loved to make up stories about the strangers she observed. The older sister was the spinster. The more somber of the two, her no-nonsense cropped hair and matching khakis flanked a shirt tucked tight enough to imagine its hospital corner ends. Lexi guessed she'd never opted to love and lose, perhaps having never loved at all.

Her kid sister, by three or four years, had entered the arena of love. This was clear from the two children, both of whom resembled their mother, "the kid sister," as Lexi had come to refer to her in her own mind. Her daughter, about fifteen, was a slender, bright-eyed fawn whose innocence was so pure it paradoxically turned her into a siren. At least so far as David was concerned. This Lexi observed.

She had a strikingly beautiful face, lit from within by childlike happiness. It was hard to determine if the brightest light came from her penetrating blue eyes, the soft rose tint of her cheeks, or the glossy, honey-blond hair that dropped to her shoulders. She had not yet lost her natural grace and spontaneity to teenage self-consciousness. At the moment, the girl was as free as a daisy swaying in a wide-open field.

Lexi watched through David's eyes. Back and forth her torso moved, as she opened plastic containers and served her family. Her snug, faded jeans didn't quite meet the bottom of her jersey top. When she stretched across the blanket to rest a filled plate in front of her aunt's perfectly aligned torso, the space widened between her shirt and her jeans, and her rosy skin shown brightly. The patch of flesh was as luminous as low-lit candles, as bright as her eyes, and as rich as her hair.

David cleared his throat, a sign that Lexi knew meant he was entering the air chamber of his emotions. The young girl gave her head a quick tilt backwards as she realigned her body and sat back on her legs. Turning forward and toward her mother, and in David's direction as well, the yearling caught her first glimpse of the forty-five-year-old man, in black sunglasses, with full, soft lips who was watching her.

Snug within the intimacies of her family, she chatted with her mother and aunt, paying close attention to her younger brother at the same time. Brimming with vitality, she complemented her family's quotidian reality.

The absence of a grown man spoke volumes about the past. Had both women been separated from their husbands, by treachery or by choice? Had their men been driven away by austerity—modest dinners, disapproving looks, and mechanical sex? Were their homes so tidy that irrationality of any sort was barred, and with it spontaneity? A slow death of that other side of life—the one with its own voracious appetites, ones that can't be extinguished. Lexi knew that part always got fed somehow, no matter what.

Frightened by the picture, Lexi wondered what the sisters accomplished by their prudent ways. Were they now ship-shape? Or had they fallen behind in the search for meaning, robbing their children of their birthright—access to a hopeful sensuality? Maybe, instead, they'd planted a wanton seed in this young girl and her brother.

While the women re-enacted the rituals of the hearth, the young boy, perhaps about nine, mimicked his elders' melancholy. Emotionally detached from the mealtime preparations, he hung over a magazine, and with heavy motions turned the pages slowly. The child seemed lost in a shadow world, with no useful male guide in sight.

Being useful—possibly crucial—made his sister cheery. She'd now engaged her aunt in conversation, smiling sweetly and moving her body rhythmically from side to side as she settled her plate on her lap. Lexi was in pain as David made some perfunctory comments to his mother while the drama unfolded. With an eye on the girl's blanket, he'd raise his arm, then bend his elbow to feign a scratch on his back. It was a familiar gesture, one Lexi had noticed long ago. This is how he could insert himself into someone else's panoramic sweep, much like a slice of celluloid footage mysteriously edited into someone else's life.

Still unconscious of all that was going on around her, the teen was now turning routinely in David's direction. He reinforced her glances with a barrage of quick tilts of his head, followed by coughs. With the weight of David's dead-on stares, the girl's movements became less fluid. Suddenly she was center stage. Oh, how Lexi remembered the feeling.

Lexi grew anxious and restless. Making forays into conversation with her mother-in-law, she was answering questions forgotten by mid-sentence. David hung back, turned away from his wife and mother.

Then the young girl gave her best performance of the day. A young man in his twenties joined them. Ah. Her cousin. So the older sister had been married after all. Lexi intuited the mother-son relationship by the way he'd largely ignored her while jovially greeting the other woman and the budding Lolita. Switching it all around, Lexi thought he might simply be the two women's much younger brother, the offspring, perchance, of their father's second wife, the one for whom he'd left Lolita's mother.

Whatever. They all loved him, fussing happily over him and stepping up their performances. The ploys triggered laughter and joy. Meanwhile, David kept his oar in. By then Lexi figured the erect nipples showing through the girl's T-shirt were more for David than the latecomer cousin-uncle.

The sense that Helen seemed unaware of the drama only intensified Lexi's pain. For Lexi, the whole scenario was an open wound that was being stretched out so quickly on all sides that she felt the whole universe might fall, and she'd be sucked into its fleshy chasm, then go under.

How she visualized this pain was so base that it was bloodless. A wound that never bled, just gaped, instead. To her, the absence of blood wiped out the chance for healing. God, she pleaded, please tell me what's wrong with him.

Mechanically, she tended to those around her. The boys had gone to get ice cream. Eventually the whole family, including David, worked as human beacons to guide the kids back to their postage-stamp-sized spot, while the parallel drama with the girl on the blanket next door continued. In the shadows, David and his teenage temptress were silently consorting in the midst of their respective families.

The seduction took place even as Lexi kept up the momentum of polite conversation with her mother-in-law, doled out dollars for ice cream to the boys, and rotely packed up the leftover food. What was left was the denouement, and only a cellist could have aptly captured her angst. The teen had left the blankets, probably to empty her bladder. David was obviously impatient awaiting her return. Now canvassing the 180-degree area that flanked the timber rest rooms, hundred of yards away, he would occasionally link eyes with Lexi, who was surveying the opposite 180-degree stretch bracketing the ice cream takeout.

If David's objective was to train her in emotional detachment—she might congratulate him on his brilliance. She was an empty soul, too stricken to feel sad. The loss blotted her out.

Infidelity needs only one partner to play, but takes everything sacred in a relationship with it. She could only imagine many such scenes in David's life, episodes that might be increasing at a geometric rate.

The Boston Symphony Orchestra might as well have been Johnny Cash with a backup of string instruments. The crescendo served only as a signal for Lexi that the exasperating, wounding, episode was over. No goose bumps or being borne into heaven on the music's wings this year. She hurriedly picked up the blankets, herding the family out amid the cheerfully rowdy crowd.

Back home, she and David were in the master bathroom, preparing for sleep. Lexi stood at one of the two sinks and was about to pick up her tube of toothpaste. She looked at David's reflection in the mirror, as he stood at the other sink, and said, "So, are you gonna maybe line her up for baby-sitting?"

"Who?"

"Miss Tanglewood. I thought you were going to trip on your tongue. I was embarrassed for you, David."

"We seem to have an issue here, but I'm not sure what the hell you're talking about."

"I saw you, David. The whole damn park saw you. Did she give you her number?"

"You should get some sleep, Lex, before it gets any crazier in here."

"You need to own this."

"What are you talking about? You're making this up."

"Talk to me, goddamnit."

"There's nothing to talk about. Now go to bed."

David sat against the carved headboard, waiting for Lexi to finish in the bathroom and come to bed. She walked toward her side of the ebony bed, shoulders back, eyes cast downward.

David pulled her toward him. "I love you, Lexi."

"I love you, David," she said kissing him woodenly, then snuggled under the blanket, pulled up her legs and shifted her body toward the wall. Hugging her pillow, Lexi prayed for help in making sense of the evening, and wondered if she could accept this new behavior as part of David's slide into mid-life.

She had a hard time getting her mother-in-law to the airport in the morning after a night of fitful sleep. David had to return to work. After she and Helen said good-bye, Lexi gave in to her exhaustion and headed home. Yanking open the console on the Jaguar, Lexi pulled out a bag of pistachios she kept handy for just such moments. The speedometer hit sixty-five miles per hour, as Lexi, shelling and nibbling the pistachios, reached for the cellular phone. Juggling the steering wheel, the nuts, and the black handle of the car phone, she sped up the second she heard Shakti's voice.

"Do you have a minute, Shakti? Something's happened."

"Sure. What's up?"

"We were at Tanglewood yesterday, and David got into a seduction routine with the girl on the blanket next to ours."

"David?"

"She was fifteen."

"How bizarre."

"Worse than that. I'm so miserable that I'll do whatever it takes to shake the pain."

"Let's have lunch."

"Okay, but what do you think I should do? Step up the schedule for plastic surgery?"

"You're getting breast implants at seventy-five. Right?"

"Yeah. By then they'll probably be safe enough. But there are other things I could do now."

"Lexi, it's the dark side. Sport plus *men*opause. They get it, too."

"It's sick."

"Just as sick as wanting one in each color."

"Stereotypes only go so far. What about the soul?"

"It holds it all," Shakti said softly, then after a long pause asked, "Did you talk to him about it?"

"Talk? I don't know. I was angry. But he said he didn't know what I was talking about. And how could I ever have made it up?"

"Lexi, he's basically a good guy. He loves you."

"Raj would never do that."

"Never say never. Plus you've aired the wound. What's the risk of letting it go?"

"That we won't need to have lunch."

"See you tomorrow."

"Armando's?'

"I'll make the reservation."

Lexi was reticent at dinner that night, holding back the ups and downs of her day. Still unapologetic, she felt sad, and could tell that David was also uncomfortable. Rob had gone to a friend's home, making the situation even more awkward.

Coming out of his cave slowly, David tried a couple of stabs at conversation before he said, "Lexi, I could move up that trip I need to make to Indonesia. We could go together and do something afterwards."

"It's just so far away," Lexi said.

"With all you've been doing lately, the plane ride will feel like a spa."

True. As a freelance strategy consultant, she'd been working with non-profits lately. It was the kind of work that gave her the greatest satisfaction right now. She was wrapping up her current project for The Boston Civic jazz program. Right now there was a natural break. The schedule for the fall was set, a major fundraising effort was under way, and most of the musicians were touring up and down the coast, or in Europe.

Yes, she could meet her other deadlines before leaving, and take some work with her. Fortunately, their lifestyle supported such spontaneity. They'd consciously avoided complicated social networks, preferring a simpler life. Both she and David earned enough money to more than meet the cost of Rob's education.

For the past six years, Lexi had also supported her nephew's special education needs, and would do so in the future, giving him the best possible vocational training. They were wealthy, but they'd avoided obvious money pits, like country clubs, yachts, and private planes. It was more satisfying, and much easier, to earmark ten percent of their income for philanthropy, and splurge on luxurious vacations.

"Could we go when Rob's at Boy Scout camp?" she asked cautiously. "That would be just over two weeks from now."

"Good idea. Maybe. Let me work on it."

"Okay. But let's make the business stop first. Then we'll have the rest of the time to ourselves," she said, a bit more energetic.

"I'll see what I can work out," he said, stroking her thigh under the table.

Lexi was eager to go back to Bali, where they'd spent their honeymoon nine years ago. For her, it was the most enchanting place in the world. But that was before they had Rob. Right now it seemed like a fantasy, far away and fragile, and she was afraid to invest her hopes in something that might feel so different now. Plus it was 15,000 miles away, and being that far from Rob gnawed at her day and night. Traveling halfway around the world was scary; if she went any further, she'd be on her way home.

Lexi liked the fact that Rob would be with his friends. He already loved camping and had gone on a lot of exciting outings this year. As the days passed, she started to believe that their separate adventures would make them each more, not less.

She had strong contacts with cultural organizations, and her reputation had spread by word of mouth. Most people in music and the arts thought about strategy last, if at all. For the most part, artistic directors, prodded by an outspoken or influential board member, would reluctantly agreed to meet with her to discuss projects. Sometimes an executive director's attitude at the beginning of a project wasn't much better. She understood the importance of a personal artistic vision, but knew any vision had the greatest impact when a group tapped the right markets for both audience and financial support. That was her specialty.

Her current project had gone well and The Boston Civic Center was committed to developing a top flight jazz program with a concert series and a broad educational program. Jazz was America's music, unforgettable and unfettered. Lexi once heard it described as "the story of a million nights when men and women of all colors came together and made great art."

After the program was launched last spring, Lexi grew more and more appreciative of the exuberant performances. The sweet, supple sounds fed her spirit. But some of her favorite memories were from the student rehearsals she and David attended. That's when Lexi got caught up in the artistic process, being in the room while young women and men developed their sound, letting loose and experimenting with great emotion. Lexi would get chills watching the eager face of a trumpet player as he picked up a line from the piano, then passed it along to the sax. Improvisation was an art, and the overwhelming message of the give and take was love.

Lexi played a Duke Ellington number in her head as she packed her suitcase. First she pulled out her most romantic garments, starting with the long white Indian skirt that Shakti had secretly stashed in her honeymoon bag. Toward the back of her closet, she found her much loved, hand-painted, turquoise silk caftan, perfect for lounging. The aquamarine hues were a lot like the ocean, and she liked knowing that everyone in the family would be by the water.

Energized by images of other retreats to exotic places, she opened drawers, scanned shelves and leafed through her hanging rack. Remembering a chiffon wraparound she'd once bought from a vendor in Barbados, she searched furtively, then plucked it from her drawer. Where was that black, strapless suit with the zebra-lined bust? Then on to the sandals that would have made Cleopatra weep.

Getting out of town was more hectic than usual. Once she knew for sure that every item on Rob's packing list was safe within his duffel and his bus had left the Scout house, Lexi tended to the final security checks at home. She'd already stopped all three newspapers and the mail, and taken sworn testimony from the gardeners and the pool maintenance team about keeping the gates to her home locked. Had life grown richer, or was it getting too complicated? The next day, as they departed, she let go of the hassles when the limo driver, instead of asking about their plane tickets, wondered if they'd remembered all their medication. Lexi was happy to be in good health.

Traveling as much as she did, Lexi believed a vacation might just as well start on the plane. And it was okay if she and David found different ways to decompress. David always held her hand on takeoff and she mentally released him of any other responsibilities until landing when he, once again, offered her his hand. Between those two points she had books, films, daydreams, music, meditation, and sleep. A flight was Lexi's opportunity to repair the damage to the senses that leaving town always caused.

Stopping in Jakarta first for business would give them time to break their jet lag before spending six precious days in Bali. Lexi would have a chance to meet some of David's colleagues, and was looking forward to a dinner at Pandji Hamad's home. Invitations to people's homes were one of her favorite parts of traveling. More intimate than gathering at a restaurant, dining *en famille* was a better way to get to know others, and their customs.

Their driver spoke into the call box of the security system at the gate to the Hamad's home. Pandji, as if to counter the unfriendly impression created by screening those who visited his home, was waiting outside the house as they pulled up, and moved quickly toward their car once they rounded the last corridor of thick bushes on the private road.

Lexi was struck by the energy of this man, just over five feet tall. His brown eyes brightened to a golden hue when he opened the door of the limousine and reached in for Lexi's hand. Pandji guided her over the gravel drive, walking her spiritedly through the carved wooden doorway of his home.

Champiung, his wife, stood just inside the compound, wearing a traditional sarong, her breasts wrapped in yellow saffron bands of cotton, covered for modesty by a lace kebaya. Lexi took Champiung's hand into hers a moment longer than typical, and held it as she looked into her eyes, sensing her pain as she absorbed her beauty. David had told Lexi of their eldest daughter's illness, and the way the ordeal had emotionally ravaged the young family.

Pandji led the way into what Lexi imagined was an Indonesian version of a family room. Rattan furniture, potted ferns, and large ceramic pots made the space casual and comfortable. Pandji introduced David and Lexi to his children, first to Dyah, just seven years old, who sat regally in a mid-sized wheelchair by the window. Lexi bowed down to shake her hand, and was charmed by her delicate face. Flanked by thick, dark hair pulled straight back and mounted high in a pony tale, her face was luminous, like a tender blossom in a thick forest.

Her brother, Sarda, five years old, stood solemnly by his parents, moving only when his mother eased him forward to greet Lexi. Lexi bowed gently toward him and repeated his name.

Pandji led the conversation, asking about their trip and the accommodations at the Sari Pacific. Lexi felt they could have been anywhere in the world getting to know a new family, until a gecko jumped down from the wall near her chair and she watched as the tiny lizard disappeared behind a pot.

The young girl reacted first and spoke softly. Her mother translated. Dyah says, "The gecko's good luck." Lexi smiled as Dyah leaned forward, revealing the pink silk cushion on her wheelchair.

Champiung giggled, nodding in support of her daughter's explanation.

Sharing Champiung's laughter, Lexi said she was fascinated by reptiles of all shapes and sizes. In fact, on their trip to Bali nine years ago she'd been photographed with a fifty-pound python around her neck. "The picture came in handy," she said, "whenever she went over her house rules about roughhousing with Rob's friends."

Dyah winced, then turned to her mother when the shrill tones of a baby's cry broke the rhythm of the conversation.

"I must excuse myself," Champiung said.

Lexi interpreted the sharp, quick sound that Dyah made to be a protest.

Champiung patted her daughter's hands, whispering to her before leaving the room.

Lexi turned quickly to speak to Dyah, and Pandji translated.

When Champiung returned, she was joined by a houseboy who called them to dinner. Pandji explained that the children would dine separately.

As they said their good-byes, Dyah instructed her father to ask Lexi if she would send pictures of her son, and promised to write him when her handwriting got better.

"Of course," Lexi said, reaching for her hand as Pandji conveyed her message. "I know he would like you."

David's eyes locked on Lexi as they walked toward the dining table. She took strength from his warmth, and the hunch that the hospital he was helping to build could make the Hamad's lives better.

David and Pandji talked about the firm's plans for the cancer center.

"It's like a dream for us," Pandji said. "Champiung went to Singapore for Dyah's first treatments six months ago. It was hard for the family to be separated. Now, with the baby, it's impossible to keep everyone together. But it will take time before we have the trained doctors and equipment here."

Champiung told Lexi that her sister might take Dyah to Singapore for the next leukemia treatment. While the hospital there had let her stay in Dyah's room at night, they would not allow the baby. The cost of taking multiple hotel rooms for the family and the servants was prohibitive.

David and Lexi's car arrived at ten o'clock to take them to the hotel. Lexi found it hard to leave and wondered how they would manage. She knew that suffering could strengthen the character of an older person, but seeing it strike someone so young was tragic. Not quite Rob's age, Dyah was a bright spirit, and Lexi prayed that her body would heal.

As they drove to the hotel, Lexi felt blessed to have met the Hamads. In the midst of the tropical palms, an eager gecko, and Dyah's wheelchair with the pink cushion, Lexi felt the power of grace knitting them together for a short but potent time. She savored those moments when she and David, together, reached beyond their family to something larger.

Lexi was proud that David had made a strong, personal commitment to Indonesia, and that, with the support of the government, the treatment center in Jakarta might help Dyah by early next year.

The next afternoon, Lexi and David were on their afternoon

flight into Bali. The airport in Denpassar was her bridge to a different way of being. The custom agents, all male, moved with the beauty and grace of dancers in an Indonesian ballet. Greeted by the soft voice of a young man who seemed to cradle her passport in his hand, she studied the slight tilt of his head and the way his lips spread to a smile as he welcomed her to Bali. His body, mostly shielded by his workstation, moved ever so subtly as he spoke, reminding Lexi of a warrior shadow puppet with shoulders twice as wide as his waist. Lexi paused to enjoy his taut, angular frame fed, she imagined, by savory bananas, jasmine rice, and spicy chunks of meat.

As their driver spoke in melodic tones about the island, the people, and their traditions on the way to the resort, Lexi felt enmeshed in an exotic dance. She spotted the fringe of the thatched roof as they pulled up to the Bali Oberoi, and she felt her body respond to its natural, sinuous lines. Easing her way down the long covered pathway to the resort, Lexi gazed at the reflections on the ponds, edged artfully by stone sculptures and wildly colorful blossoms. She felt as integral to the magic of the place as the bamboo columns lashed against the thatched roof.

A man named Wayang, dressed in a gold tunic, bowed to welcome her, raising and lowering his hands as he offered his blessings. Lexi merged with the beauty of the encounter. All of this brought the Balinese spirit into her soul.

Lexi threaded her arm around David's back as Wayang guided them to their private bungalow. She'd heard that the entrance to a Balinese home was considered a gateway to the occupant's soul. As they entered, they moved easily through a rose-colored, sandstone archway. Once in the courtyard, Wayang unhooked a wooden mallet next to the door and tapped three times to cleanse the house of evil spirits.

Passing by the lily pond nestled next to the bungalow, Lexi followed David inside their abode. Her eyes rested on the small, dark wood ladders meant to ease their climb up to the bed, centered on a raised platform. The bedroom seemed lofty, a castle overlooking a kingdom.

Outside, behind the bungalow, was a courtyard with an eight-foot wall that gave boundaries to their Balinese Eden. Male and female statues, each cloaked in fresh frangipani blossoms, adorned a wide, rectangular tub, centered in the space. Lexi wanted to stay here, with David, forever—to become Balinese.

"Hey, lotus blossom," David said, teasing her. "Do you feel as though you've come home?"

"Yes, I do," Lexi said as she twirled around, stretching out her spine, rotating her shoulders. "How did you know?"

Without waiting for a response, she sidled over to David and wrapped her arms around his neck, moistening his lips in a long kiss. Dissolving into a full body hug, she pressed against David's chest and pelvis, using her arms to lash them together like two columns of bamboo, bound for the long haul.

David rocked his pelvis back and forth and slid his hand down Lexi's back, fondling her buttocks. As he slipped his fingers down her pants, he inched back, in order to bring his hand around front to her pubis. Lexi's wet labia made him hard.

"You look like the bird of paradise," he whispered.

"I'd love to be that free," she said with a smile, working to unfasten his zipper, then his pant buttons.

"The freedom's just over there," he said, tilting his head toward the stairway that led up through the bath and into the bedroom.

"I'll come to you in a minute," she replied softly, trying to recollect where she'd left her purse. Experience had taught Lexi to carry her diaphragm in her pocketbook. Every time she packed it there, she'd laugh at the image of the two of them pawing though an open suitcase just off the luggage carousel at LaGuardia. Years ago, they'd hunted frantically, like dogs digging for a bone, until they found the genital-colored container.

Getting herself ready for David in the niche between their garden courtyard and their dark, rich private quarters, she imagined herself a Balinese dancer. Reminded of the memories from their honeymoon here, she moved through her ritual in a trance-like state, offering her lovemaking to Siwa, the Balinese god of creation.

David bypassed the small ladder to the bed and stretched out in the raised bed, lying quietly like a lion. On his back, hands clasped behind his head, he studied the intricate patterns on the ceiling. He began to stroke himself, studying the room. The Balinese believed eight points of latitude anchored the world, and his eyes were drawn to the center of the ceiling where a handsome carved rose was set. The Rose Wind was in the ninth direction. The center of the universe. The core.

David heard Lexi climb the steps to their room, and focused on her eyes, only peripherally aware of the way her breasts moved gently from side to side in the snug blue chiffon cloth tied around her body. Her eyes were unusually intense. Their pale green clarity always hooked his soul. It didn't matter whether he was upbeat, distracted, or agitated. His connection to her started with her eyes.

But whenever her eyes darkened, he was afraid. Each time it laid bare his deep, half-buried, desire to please. David longed to build bridges to those he loved, mostly Lexi and Rob. The problems surrounding his firm's rapid growth kept him away from them. To make sense of his life, he needed to be at peace with his family. Lexi taught him that if he could relax into the flow of the family, open his heart to its beauty, he'd be rejuvenated. Life could be hard or it could be easy. He had the power to choose.

Lexi put one bare foot above the other, using the small wooden ladder to join him. The center split in her garment opened as she slid in next to him, and his eyes fixed on her shapely inner thigh. As she pulled the garment up from behind her bottom, it opened and exposed her pubic hair, which was the same rich brown as the Balinese bed.

Bypassing their usual chitchat, he reached over and pulled the end of the tassel that tied her wrap together in the front, tugging down the layers of fabric to exchange chiffon for her milk-bottle white breast.

David's eyes fixed on hers. As if inflamed by her seductive pose—thick lips angling forward with shoulders back, breasts uncovered—he watched intently as she pulled the left side of her covering down below her waist. She probably would have wiggled out of it altogether, if he hadn't moved forcefully between her legs. His hands gave way to his mouth, and he sucked her nipples until they reached for the sky.

Lexi opened her eyes, and caught a glimpse of his face—so clear and content. As her expression softened, they merged, and she felt a charge run through his body. He squeezed her flesh; she felt it pulse in his palm. A passionate aura surrounded them, rising in all directions from their bodies. Journeying down below her fertile mound of flesh, David stopped just below her belly, the route to her creativity. It was as though raw sexual energy fueled him.

Still in a trance, Lexi loosened her knees and spread her legs wide as David brushed his mouth over her fringed entrance to eternity. Opening the gateway to her soul, Lexi heard David whisper, "My own Rose Wind."

Feeling her moist labia thicken, Lexi imagined the two large petals as the Rose Wind. Did their shape issue from the wind and water of evolution? Or, perhaps, the hands, tongues, and cocks of those who came before?

Lexi felt as beautiful as a tender rose as David touched her temple of creation. And as David played with her first speck of moisture, she opened up, as mighty as a desert flower at dawn. Then Lexi quieted herself as David moved his tongue through her fleshy gates. Feeling like the bird of paradise, she tingled when he placed his lips over her stiff, pulpy wedge and feverishly sucked her sweetness. Lexi felt as though she were hurtling through space, then left the stratosphere on angel wings. Breathing was her safety belt. Heaving, she held on. Her belly was her guide, storing then releasing vital essences as she went.

David's mouth drove twinges deep within her core.

Her hips clenched when she could take no more, and David responded to the cue, dropping back with gentle licks. Steadying herself as she looked down on his curly crown, she knew this was but a pause. And Lexi stayed still, like an overripe melon that yearned to be finished off.

Twisting and turning as David fixed on a sucking motion that brought her to her second peak, she writhed from one cardinal direction to the next. Splayed out on the bed, she felt like a poem. So tender. Real. Honest. Lexi basked in the moment.

David paused, then in guttural tones said, "Again, lotus blossom, we're going to come again."

Would it be speed? Pressure? As David moved the palm of his hand in circles over her pelvis, Lexi wondered where he would take her next.

He placed his mouth back on her fleshy, salmon-colored Rose Wind, and he built momentum. Lexi's pelvis lurched forward and she let out an ethereal wail. Like a siren beckoning him closer, despite dangerous waters, she wanted it all. Lexi's world broke open as David, harder still and eager for his own release, stayed the course.

She couldn't resist the rhythm he'd created, nipping her clitoris lightly yet rapidly, his finger tapping in and out between two mountains of vanilla flesh. Then he raised the stakes. Unable to distinguish his fiery mouth from his torrid hands, Lexi flipped forward like earth thrown upwards in a quake. Her sounds shifted from the lilting cries of angels to survival pants. Lexi's mountain spring broke loose, turning her waterfall into a river rapid. Whitecaps of passion slapped against his mouth, and David sped up the ride.

Just when Lexi felt most indomitable, her fury broke. Calling out to him and to God, in phrases and tones that an ornithologist would simply label joy, Lexi's body rocked like the evolutionary wind of change.

That's when she noticed the wildness in his eyes as he bore down and moved inside her. All she could offer was a narrow passageway. Her tissues, swollen to the max, were but a tight corridor. Had he ever felt harder? His cock spiked the slender channel in a split-second. The sensation consumed her, setting off her loudest, freest cries. Lexi rebounded as he knifed through her body, expecting him to come out the other side.

Or maybe she would go under. Cycling down to her geyser's center, she lost control. As centrifugal force sucked her under, she caught a glimpse of the carved Rose Wind. Then Lexi wailed as those never ending spirals pulled her toward the center of the earth.

Awakened early by the roosters, Lexi and David planned to head to Peliatan and arrive by midday to watch one of the best dance troupes on the island. Lexi mused as she got herself ready for the outing. Sunscreen. Wraparound sunglasses with a pink, stretchy strap that hugged her temples. Her multi-colored, Guatemalan fanny pack. She was traveling light.

Driving north, they passed miles of rice paddies, lit like shallow lakes by the early morning glow. The tiny shafts of rice poked through the still, greenish-brown water that covered large parcels of land. For Lexi, time stopped when she took in the image. With oxen yoked together, workers planted the glistening paddies as they had for centuries. They walked the oxen slowly through the still water, making furrows in the paddies. She felt as though the morning light etched the timeless scene in her memory.

At the temple in Peliatan, there was a procession of women carrying baskets of fruit on their heads, walking beside their children, as synchronized and rhythmic as dancers. The bright colors of fruit, the plates of temple food, and the floral offerings to the gods added luster to the procession. Watching the younger women, she doubted that any one of them would stray from her concentration to respond to a man's advances, like the teenager at Tanglewood.

David and Lexi chose seats toward the left side of the temple courtyard and relaxed as they watched the villagers gather. The Balinese moved gracefully and with purpose. The process of assembling for the ceremony felt a lot like the initial stage of a meditation. Lexi joined in the ritual. Her breathing slowed and she began to focus. Soon she let her mind go. She could tell that others did, too. Lexi could feel a certain power take hold, much like a group meditation, and she sensed that the dance would begin because people were ready for it to start.

Opening the simple program she'd been given at the gate, Lexi read that the dalang, a man named Samal, would begin the ceremony. The spiritual leader of the group, he was seated on the floor in the middle of the gamelan, an Indonesian orchestra.

There was a hush so silent it seemed to be sound as he opened his mouth to offer incantations to the gods. As the last guttural sound wafted from his turban-wrapped head, the celestial tones of the gamelan's brass pots tinkled like bells.

Lexi looked out at the orchestra of twelve men sitting cross-legged, each behind one of the different-sized brass pots. Two drummers, whose instruments were covered in black-and-white-checkered cloth to repel the evil spirits, began to beat out a tempo that rippled through the temple.

Mesmerized by the entrance of a young girl tightly wrapped in layers of metallic silk, Lexi's heart quickened as she watched the dancer's subtle motion. Gradually shifting her weight, the legong invoked the blessings of the gods, then moved into a trance. Her faraway look and still mouth seemed to plumb the deepest recesses of the soul. The dance, Lexi knew, was meant to bring both audience and dancers to a different way of being.

As the girl's supple neck moved slowly from side to side, Lexi felt her own consciousness start to change. She felt lighter and freer. Suspending all thoughts, Lexi started to gently sway in time with the clinking of the gamelan's tiny brass pots. Within moments, Lexi could feel the dancer's movements in her own body.

Captivated by the beauty of the legong's heavy gold head-dress, cut like filigree with intricate patterns reminiscent of ancient times, Lexi settled into rich fantasies of her own. It was as though the fresh frangipani blossoms that stocked the young woman's crown adorned Lexi's head as well. And as she imagined five sets of her own bare arms cycling through the erotic dance positions, like the goddess Siwa, she became one with the dance.

Lexi toggled back and forth between her inner world and the stage as the legong recalled the timeless struggle of good and evil. She enjoyed watching the eleven-year-old girl take on the role of different characters as she knit together the critical part of a woman's journey—the passage from maiden to queen. Lexi thought of how she'd been lured by her own lusty desires as she sought enduring love.

The maiden is threatened when an evil king finds her lost in the forest. The daughter of a rival ruler, she becomes a pawn in his quest for power. Her father pleads for her freedom. But instead, her captor tries to strike a bargain with his young prisoner: submit to him and he'll spare her father the agony of war. Stalwart, the virgin rejects him. Heroically her family organizes troops to fight for their daughter's release.

Exploring the complexity of the divided woman's struggle, two young girls dramatize the conflict with the malevolent ruler. They stretch out their limbs like petals to repel the king's seductive advances. Stamping their feet with fury, they flutter their fans at high speeds. The bells, mirrors, and colored stones that overlay their costumed torsos add magical power as their courage builds.

Passionately, they pulse in self-defense. Imitating the elusive spin of hummingbirds, the two girls mirror each other's rapid movements. Faster and faster until they break into a spin. Much like the illusion of finely crafted cartoon animation, they create a pattern. Hands, lips and, torsos twitch rapidly as their bodies move in fluid circles. Twirling furiously, they become one beautiful golden orb and their legs, arms, and heads merge, as if with centrifugal force. They become still.

Wondrous. Centered in their own beliefs, the maidens triumph—their innocence intact. The older male is defeated in his attempt to rob them of their childhood. Triumphant, the girls keep their beauty and their power. Winding in and out of the circle, the legongs stamp their feet, as vibrations of victory flow throughout the temple garden.

Samal, the dalang, watches the girls celebrate sensuality on their own terms. As the spiritual teacher, his job is coming to a close. The dancers play out the wisdom of the Balinese culture where young girls are taught to experience their god-given passion at an early age. As the medium, the dalang has had the role of making sure the dance centers and stills them. The threat of sexual theft teaches them to define their boundaries. Samal's face relaxes and his smile broadens as the purifying dance continues. The maidens become the dance as the community looks on. Through this initiation, they learn to love on their own terms.

"That was remarkable," David said. "Though, I must confess, I really didn't know what was going on."

Lexi's laughter brought them together. Then she said, "I think it was about the essence of a woman's struggle. How easily the girl might have mistaken the king for the other. A father image. And he was willing to trade on the resemblance, but she woke up. Made herself conscious."

"Then what?"

"Then the rest of her life. That's why the community helps girls define their boundaries early. It's beautiful."

"I felt so motionless at times," David said, "yet without checking out, mentally or physically. It was the opposite, actually."

"Did it feel magical?"

"Maybe. Whatever that means."

"I think that's when we get closer to our unconscious."

"Could be."

"That's what wakes us up. Then the real relationship can begin. You know I was thinking about Dyah, too, at that point. Wondering if she'd ever learn the dance."

"The Hamad's daughter?"

"David, we need to help her. Them. Her whole family."

"That's why I like working here. There's so much we can do."

"Yes, like provide better health care," said Lexi.

When they returned from the dance there was a message waiting for David from his partner. A snag in the medical center project. David wanted to keep the problem from intruding on their new happiness.

As Lexi ran the water in their garden tub, he returned Jason's call. "I got your message," David said. "What's changed?"

That was all Lexi heard of the conversation. She didn't think too much about it. This was their vacation. If he had a crisis at work, she knew he'd tell her. They did everything together.

David was irked by the intrusion. "What's the problem?" he asked, looking for a way to make it disappear.

"The money," Jason said emphatically. "Suharto's folks say it's a temporary problem. But they need our help."

"What do they want us to do?"

"Come up with thirty percent of the debt as collateral."

"That will cost us. Interest rates are high now."

"David. This is a chance for us to get in on the deal. Maybe we could raise it internally. Make it part equity, part debt, to cut the risk. Give the partners a shot at equity stakes. The government will pay interest on the debt portion, and those of us in the firm will end up ahead, without losing the hospital project."

"So, we won't just be building the hospital, we'll be investors, too." He thought about how much Lexi would like that. "You're right. We need to see the project through. It means a lot to the people here. And Suharto will keep us whole."

Finished with her preparations, Lexi lowered herself into the garden tub set in the corner of the private walled courtyard behind their bungalow. Borrowing a frangipani blossom from the statue of the Balinese goddess on the ledge next to her, she adorned herself. Playfully, Lexi mimicked the way the dancer moved her body when she first realized she was lost in the forest. Enjoying the sensations, she lost track of time.

David's voice brought her back into the moment. "We're blessed, lotus blossom," he said as he stepped into the outdoor tub.

Leaning forward, she reached over to tickle him between the legs and said with a lilt, "Yes. I think we found the essence of this place today."

"And yesterday," he said with a wide smile.

"Definitely yesterday," she said, happy to feel him drape his arms around her.

Like two spoons stacked together, they rocked from side to side in the warm water.

"It's so lush here," Lexi said. "And complex."

"I can't remember which sociologist came up with the concept that the character of a people is molded most by the landscape around them."

"Sounds familiar. Everyone here is gorgeous. Especially the women. Warm. Graceful. Balanced. And so thin and shapely. Even women my age."

Gently guiding her chin toward him, David said in heartfelt tones, "Do you know that I couldn't enjoy your body more than I do?"

With a smile, Lexi said, "Probably not."

"It's true. You'll always be my temptress, Lexi. And my muse. And now I know you're a goddess," David said, piling her curls on top of her head.

"David, I'm so glad we came here," she said, stroking his face.

"Me, too," he said, kissing the nape of her neck.

Lexi moved closer.

Lightly running her tongue inside the edge of David's ear, she lingered when she reached the center.

Squeezing her tightly, he said, "Look at those stars."

"Like flecks of the finest crystal."

"So clear."

"That's how I feel about everything now."

"Yes."

Holding David's face between her slender hands, Lexi said, "I love you, David. Coming here makes that clear."

"I'll follow you anywhere Lexi, but ..."

"How about in there?" Lexi asked, motioning toward their room.

Rising as if in one motion, they stood in the middle of their garden bath, safe in the thick, moist air, tinged with fragrant blossoms.

"Do you want to see if we're as good as those dancers?" she teased, as she did a slow dance.

"No contest," David said, mirroring her move.

They stood still, arms wrapped round each other.

"We've come home," Lexi murmured.

AUTUMN

We never know how high we are
Till we are called to rise
And then, if we are true to plan
Our statures touch the skies

                                      ~ EMILY DICKINSON

L ike a videocamera, Lexi's eyes panned the Napa Valley
mountain vineyard. The late September sun, low in the
sky, beat down on rows of well-tended vines, pregnant
now with cabernet grapes. The plump fruit hung, swollen with
juice. Kneeling down and cupping a triangle of them in her
palm, Lexi sniffed the spray. Instinctively, she brought the purple cluster to her lips and flicked one into her mouth. The skin
broke as she tongued the grape against the top of her mouth.
Then she took in a deep breath of mountain air. The sweetness
stung.

   With the California sun on her back, Lexi glanced up at
David as the light danced across his eyes. Rising from the
ground, she asked, "How about a taste?" And as the juice
roamed around her mouth, Lexi pressed her moist lips against

his. She teased his tongue into her mouth and massaged it with the soft flesh of the grape. Fragrant and slow, the kiss oozed with tenderness. Molding her lips around David's like soft clay, Lexi created a passage. Their tongues swirled around the crevices of what felt like one mouth. Consummating the rare tastes, they lingered, voluptuously rubbing against each other.

Turning toward the sun, Lexi looked up at the mountain. The whole vineyard felt mystical. As did the bond she, David, and a higher power shared. She wondered if the Benedictine monks had this connection between God and man in mind when they pioneered the art of wine-making four centuries before.

David had arranged this weekend at the Diamond Mountain vineyard to celebrate their twenty-fifth anniversary. Lexi was grateful that her life had come together in so many important ways. With Rob and his new family just an hour's drive away, the clan felt more intact than ever. Her work continued to support her life, rather than the reverse. Helping arts organizations kept her vital, even stoked her soul. Passing on hard-won knowledge felt good, and working from home on a project basis made sense. Her specialty was helping clients sort out market segments for their products, and grow their businesses strategically. Lexi was awed by her luck, and often thought of Georgia O'Keeffe, who believed that it's not where you've been that matters, but what you've done with where you've been.

Early that morning she'd gotten up to work on some tough issues facing a long-term client. Having built the most exciting live theater company in Boston, the Prism Theater was faced with more competition than ever. Lexi had helped them define competition in a new way, and that included anything people might choose to do for entertainment. The list was bigger than ever. New movie theaters were showing more independent and art films than in the past, and there were more and more blockbuster concert tours, as well as the local staple of ever-popular sports events. One key issue was whether people were spending more money overall on entertainment. And, were they making entertainment decisions closer to an outing, thus gravitating to choices that required less advanced planning?

The Prism Theater had a number of options to strengthen their subscriber base. Cycling through them now, Lexi's eyes drifted toward the top of the highest hill in the vineyard, and she felt hopeful. She looked over at David, happy to be together, with time to muse.

She and David had turned an empty nest into a cocoon. At times, their boundaries merged like grapes tossed into a vat when they were ripe enough to ferment into fine wine. They understood each other's differences as well. And their knack for connecting had never been stronger.

Woven of varied colors, David and Lexi's relationship was like a tapestry of tempered beauty and complex desire. Lexi was awed by what she'd come to know as muted passion. It was a tranquil energy that resonated from deep within her body. And it was constant. Fed by memories and reflection, by pain and by joy, her feelings for David were laced together with unbreakable strands of love and acceptance. Still, Lexi loved to be independent.

Lost in thought, she heard him speaking to her, and his voice brought her back.

"Hey, lover," he said, "if we pick up our tracks, we could be sipping some of this sooner rather than later."

"You're on," she said smiling, and started to trot down the path in the direction of the cottage.

David fell in beside her, and Lexi enjoyed the slow rhythm of two bodies, side by side, moving together at about the height of the thick trellises to their right and left. The sound of rubber-

soled feet on dry earth lingered in her memory long after she
was back in the stone cottage dressing for dinner.

Awakened by a muffled noise the next morning, Lexi roused
herself. David, no longer at her side, was in the bathroom. The
sound, she realized, was David coughing. Unrestrained at first,
the cough trailed off. Dry, hacking noises followed. The tones
reverberated in Lexi's ears. She knew something was different,
and it bothered her.

Moving to his side, she said, "What's wrong?"

"Probably nothing. I've just been run-down."

"You sound terrible."

"I know. This has dragged on since August."

"Well, it's a lot worse now."

"I'll get it checked it out."

"You promise?"

"Yes. It's gotten annoying."

"I'm sure it's nothing. Just another one of those weird viruses."

"Who knows?"

David had a difficult task ahead of him next week and didn't
need any more distractions. He'd been working with his firm's
executive committee over the past two months to solve some
tough problems in Asia. Since the firm's decision would have a
substantial impact on him personally, he had taken himself out
of the final vote last week. In the end, he'd agreed to accept the
solution proposed by the members of the governing board, and
would support the decision fully in front of the whole partnership. Nevertheless, the upcoming annual partners' meeting
would be his toughest ever.

The weekend was a welcome break. Part of David's professional success had to do with his ability to focus on present
needs, and filter out what, at the time, he deemed unimportant
to the work or pleasure at hand. This was his anniversary and he
was grateful to spend it with the woman he loved.

◦⟶

After kicking off his firm's annual meeting on Tuesday morning, David delegated the regional reports to his management team, the group leaders for Europe, Asia, Australia, South America, and the U.S. David found a seat toward the back of the large auditorium at their headquarters, hoping to physically as well as emotionally separate himself from the report that would impact him the most.

Wayne Dietrich, Director of the Asian Group, walked to the podium. Using a laser pointer to refer to the bar charts on the screen, he began.

"Overall, growth has been strong. Revenue is up twenty-eight percent from last year, averaging twenty-three percent over the last five years." The junior partners seemed particularly pleased, nodding and smiling at one another.

"However," Dietrich continued, "while political upheaval is not uncommon in Asia, we are shocked by the turn of events in Indonesia. Suharto is out, and the new government will not honor the loans to Adler, LaSalle and Thomas. This will also affect the equity investments several partners made in the project. At the end of our session on Thursday, we will vote on a number of issues. The question of how to handle the losses to our firm and our partners will be among them."

David sat calmly at the back of the room, watching his colleagues shift in their seats. He felt an odd relief after weeks of looking for a solution to the problem. If the partnership decided not to cover the individual partners' investments in Adler, LaSalle and Thomas's Indonesian projects, the outcome would be personally devastating to him.

At the break, Shakti sought David out. He had trouble looking at her.

"I'm sorry," she said, gently touching his shoulder. "That's an awfully tough break."

"Please don't mention anything to Lexi."

"She doesn't know?"

"Well, there was no reason . . .it seemed like a technicality at the time."

"David, you need to tell her. And I mean right now."

David was uncomfortable at home over the weekend, filling his time with small errands and watching more football on television than usual. On Sunday, after brunch and his usual walk with Lexi, the two of them read in the family room.

Lexi looked up from the report she was reading when David crossed the room for a second time. He stood motionless at the picture window, staring out at the backyard.

"Are you mad at me or something?" Lexi asked.

"For God's sake. Can't I just relax around here?"

"No, there's something different. Lately, anyway."

"That active imagination of yours."

"Intuition, maybe."

"So that makes you right?"

"It makes me wonder."

"What are you reading?"

"Work stuff. The annual report from the Boston Community Trust. Is that why you're mad? About Ron?"

"Who?"

"Ron Abrahms. He heads the trust now."

"Oh?"

"Yes."

"Why would I be mad about Ron Abrahms?"

"Because he's an old boyfriend."

"He is?"

"Hello. I'm Lexi Morgan. Have we met?"

"For Christ's sake."

Lexi was still staring straight at David.

"Lexi, there's something I need to tell you." David tried modulating his voice, then broke into a dry cough. He looked pale.

"What's wrong?"

"I'm going to the doctor Monday."

"Good. Did you feel any better last week?"

"No."

"I'm sorry," Lexi said as she got up and walked to him. Massaging his shoulders, she said, "Was there something else, David?"

"No, Lexi."

On Wednesday, David saw his internist. To rule out pneumonia, he agreed to get a chest X-ray. He didn't think much about it. Lexi scheduled a bone density test for the same morning. Diligent in managing her health, she had the tests annually and was about due.

Backing out of the driveway early on the morning of the tests, Lexi enjoyed seeing so many trees, particularly maples, ablaze with color. Even now the sturdy maple leaves reminded her of children's handprints. She decided that as soon as her granddaughter, Allison, was old enough, she would teach her how to iron the leaves between sheets of wax paper to preserve their beauty.

When they arrived at Mass General, Lexi sensed David's resistance. Once in the X-ray waiting room, she took out the newspaper and read him snippets of news articles. He scanned the room, paying little attention to her words.

Putting the paper down, Lexi said, "It's better to be safe."

"I'm fine," David said, as he stroked her shoulder.

"I think you're terrific," Lexi said with a smile.

"Yes, and lung cancer is very rare," he said, mentioning the unspeakable for the first time.

"I know," Lexi replied, able to contain the moment.

"How did I get so lucky?" David said in a lighter tone, putting his arm around her and pulling her close to him.

"Karma. Plus being a good person," Lexi said, as she squeezed his thigh.

"Lexi, there's something we haven't had a chance to talk about," he said.

"I think you're probably fine too, sweetheart. Truly," she said.

"It's not related to this," David said.

"You mean the way you surprised me last night?" Lexi whispered.

"Babe, I'm serious now."

"You sure felt serious last night," she teased.

"This isn't easy," he said and paused. "There's something about the partnership we should have discussed."

"Okay," Lexi said, settling down and crossing her hands in her lap.

"Remember when we added the cancer center to the medical complex in Indonesia about fifteen years ago?"

"The Suharto deal? Sure," she said.

"There was competition for the bid. And financing was tight."

"But the government was behind it," she said, mystified.

"Yes. But the Asian financial markets went to hell then. Remember?"

"What's your point?" she asked, somewhat anxious.

"We offered equity interests to partners at Adler, LaSalle and Thomas."

"So we invested?"

"I had to."

"I don't understand. We do everything together. That's our modus operandi."

"I know."

"Where did we get the money?"

"I used the house as collateral," he said in confessional tones.

"How could you?" Lexi said sharply, feeling a deep, swift cut of betrayal.

"You get so upset about the firm sometimes."

"Because you put it first," she explained in gritty, passionate tones.

"Lexi, the investment's gone bad. Suharto ruled with an iron hand for thirty years. Then everything changed."

"How much did we lose?" she asked, crossing her arms in front of her chest.

"I don't know yet. A million for the house. Now I hear there's going to be a suit by some of the partners that could cost us more." His voice weakened. "We could be wiped out."

"Jesus, David. How could you?"

"Look, I thought it was like putting money into Fort Knox."

"So, who am I? Bella Lugosi?"

"Sometimes I think you see the firm as another woman."

"Christ. Another woman would have been cheaper," she said, shaking her head.

David looked her in the eye and said, "I'm sorry."

Still petulant, Lexi said, "Me, too. What else should I know?"

"Nothing. Honestly," he said, as he reached for her hands.

"What an odd word," she said, holding back.

"Remember, Lexi. We don't know exactly why Dyah's leukemia went into remission, but maybe the center helped."

Stooped over, Lexi nodded, rubbing her forehead.

"Can we get beyond this?" David asked, as the nurse opened the door to the waiting room and called him for the X-ray.

"Somehow," Lexi whispered, feeling she'd gone numb.

Lexi got up about five o'clock the next morning to get a jump on the day. Heading upstairs to her home office with a glass of chocolate soy and a pot of coffee, her mind leapt ahead to her current project, and her pace quickened.

Setting the tray down just inside the door, she tended to her morning rituals. After switching on a small red Italian lamp, she raised her long arms toward the ceiling, then brought them straight down as she lowered her right leg to the floor, then back toward the wall. Up on her toes, with palms pressed against the floor as though she were doing a push up, Lexi sank back on her knees, stretching like a cat. Each morning her salute to the sun, plucked from yoga, centered, then unleashed, her spirit.

Writing three quick pages in her journal cleansed both her mind and emotions. She could dispense with yesterday's leftovers and lighten today's load by just moving her pen as rapidly as possible over the pages. Whether Lexi let her angst loose, toyed with a fantasy, or brainstormed solutions to a problem, journaling always opened up her world.

Pulling out her project files, Lexi could feel her heart pulse. Skimming through folders, she figured out where she'd left off before her client meeting. Tension built as she took on the toughest issues. How could the Prism Theater turn eighty percent of their customers into subscribers? What could they do differently that would make people want to see each play they produced in a season? Her mind whirred as she roughed out options on her notepad. As she built momentum, sentences turned to phrases. Then images. By the end of the brainstorming, she captured the essence of the question. Now, she'd need to layout options for her client.

Drafting memos and presentations always galvanized her to action. The immediacy gripped. She felt energy course through her. Intense. Alive. Lexi felt lighter and more insightful as she wrote. Riding herd over a host of thorny business issues, Lexi massaged them into opportunities. The muse served her well.

At a crossroads, she looked up. Full of wonder, Lexi reviewed the material. Feeling more complete, she relaxed. Looking out the window, she leaned back in her red burgundy ergonomic chair, rocking gently as she got her bearings. It was as though she was using her whole body to get from one point in the project to the next. Wide-eyed, she fixed on the sturdy pine, yards from her study. A new rush of sensations urged her forward.

Merging with the green pine needles outside her window, she swayed slightly, watching them move in the breeze. A dull ache took her to the next phase. She would not think about David's betrayal, nor his health just now. Writing faster, she finished drafting the memo outlining a new strategy for her client.

The drafting stage, where creative energies peaked, was most like riding a wild horse. All she had to do was stay on. Then, when her energies peaked, she stopped and regrouped.

Pausing, Lexi reflected. Fresh from the chaos, she breathed easily. Glancing out at the trees, she first saw them up close, then looked past them, at about the same time that the next idea came to her.

The stream of ideas flowed steadily. Once she found the process scary. Now she managed it easily. Her experience. The success. Lots of practice. Lexi believed that, at some level, creative fervor always led to important discoveries. In every instance, it was the same question. How to balance the terror of creating with the wonder of creating?

Lexi was happy to be doing work that mirrored images that came from her soul in dreams and meditations. Images of love and compassion. Mystery and grace. The sense of being in the midst of a more caring world, and images of peace.

She felt lucky to have been working with The Prism Theater for six years. The group had already produced many plays that explored the depth of the soul. Lexi was going to recommend that they create a competitive advantage now by only choosing plays that promised people transcendent moments.

When she first discussed the idea with Bertran Nathan, the

artistic director, he was struck by how right it would feel to make this the essence of their artistic mission. He knew that mature theatergoers were tired of pat, predictable plays. Bertran had also noticed how younger audiences appreciated works that were intricate, unusual, even disturbing. Perhaps, if he focused exclusively on plays that created awe and a kind of communion for his audience, he'd turn more people into long-term subscribers. That's why he went into theater in the first place: to create the room for wonder and hope in people's lives. He'd always wanted to delight audiences, but it had become more important to him lately to let them feel awe when they left the theater.

Lexi believed it was because she'd spent so much time trying to understand Bertran's beliefs, that she'd surfaced the strategy. Years ago, she'd slowed down, and learned to mine her imagination. That's when she began to center her life. And lately, she started using a similar technique to create transcendent moments. It was her love of the sensual that helped connect her to the divine. By closely following her senses, she saw the beauty in life more clearly each day, and it made her peaceful.

She had the epiphany last summer, working in her garden at dawn. She'd noticed that, ever since that moment, ordinary life had more luster. Breakfast with David had a different rhythm. Somehow their communication felt richer, often funnier, sometimes more tender. Music had the same effect on her. John Coltrane put her in a serene mood, and she listened to his CDs as she drove into Boston for meetings with clients. She noticed the way she'd take her emotions deep within her body, then release them. That was when Lexi felt centered and could explore business options from all angles.

Lexi printed out her draft. Holding the piece in her hand, she felt brighter. More complete than before. Tingling, ever so subtly, she was happy in a new way.

Early that evening, Lexi was wrapping up a call with Bertran when she heard David's car pull in.

"Lexi, are you upstairs?" he called from the foyer.

"Yes, I'm working. Come on up."

Lexi sensed his anxiety as soon as he walked into her office.

"There's a shadow on the lung," he said slowly, as his head tilted to the side. "A tumor of some sort. But it might not be malignant." A pause. "There's only one way to find out."

"Surgery?"

"Yes. It's too big to treat any other way."

"I'm so sorry, darling."

"It's my own fault. All those goddamn cigarettes. Do you know how fast people die once this starts?"

"And how long John Wayne lived."

"You know, this is crazy. I almost don't want you to be optimistic."

"Not yet. There's a lot to do right now."

Lexi put her arms around David and gave him a full body hug.

"Oh, Lexi," he whispered.

As Lexi lit the candles for dinner, she remembered so many other crises they'd weathered together. That was what she needed to focus on. Answers came slowly, if at all. It was the process of asking the questions and sorting and exploring the options that mattered. That was how they had always gotten through difficult times, and gained more clarity. It was the only way. When one was needy, the other was sturdy. That was how she would be right now, no matter how terrified she felt.

After dinner was over and the table cleared, Lexi slipped her arm around David's waist and squeezed him tightly. Then gave him a whimsical smile.

"I don't think I can," he said.

"You don't have to. I just want to touch you."

"Okay," he said, looking more relaxed.

Lexi undressed slowly in her walk-in closet, then slipped into a pair of sheer pajamas. The peach chiffon V-neck top was pretty. Long enough to hide the elasticized waist on the pants, the pajama top had clean lines and was comfortable. Wrapping herself in a Thai silk robe that tied at the waist and looked like pale parchment paper, she was ready to soothe his spirits.

She lit candles. First the gold ones on the wrought-iron stand by the window, then the ivory beeswax candles on the ledge over the king-size bed. Lexi had this ritual in mind when David roughed out the architectural drawings for the recessed shelf. Along with the candles was a tiny, delicate, Oriental screen, and Lexi took comfort in the artwork's spring motif, painted thick with peach blossoms—an Asian good-luck symbol.

Opening the antique walnut armoire she and David had bought in France, Lexi took inspiration from the deep, vivid carvings. With its curved crown top, it was a standout. Adorned with French symbols of the wedding feast—birds hovering over a basket filled with flowers—the effect was joyous. Over the years, she and David carefully put many good things into the basket of their marriage, and it breathed easily, like the French wicker on the armoire.

More compelling was the way they cherished each other. As she reached in the cabinet to select a CD, Lexi knew a piano concerto would be just right. Chopin was one of their favorites. She thought of the composer as her friend right now, and knew that he'd give her the extra help she needed.

Lifting the massage oil from the Ojai Valley Spa off the tray in the cabinet, Lexi thought about how much she and David enjoyed the natural splendor of the California hideaway.

When everything was set, she went to find David, and guessed he'd be at his desk. Lifting his forearm, she said, "We're all ready."

He turned his head slowly and, avoiding eye contact, rose from his brown swivel desk chair.

Once in the bedroom, he placed his terry cloth robe down by the bed, just the way he always did, and lay down on the sheets.

"Please, just relax, darling," Lexi said. "This is my turn to play."

The music lifted the energy in the room, and Lexi dripped the massage oil into her palm. Lying beside him, she spread the jasmine-scented oil generously over his chest, starting just under his neck. Light at first, the pressure built. Using long, smooth strokes, circular around his pecs, she created a rhythm. Her hand went down the side of his body, just skirting his pelvis, all the way to his feet. Lexi pressed hard on his quadriceps, easing up around the knees. Applying more oil, she ran her hand inside his thigh. Then Lexi spread out David's legs and nestled between them. She moved her fingers in time with the concerto, and watched his cock thicken. Looking up, she savored the wide smile that spread across David's face. Eyes closed and at rest, he looked peaceful.

Edging down to the end of the bed, she worked his feet, the way she'd learned in Asia. She knew that all the meridians of the body have endpoints there. By massaging the feet, she could touch all of his organs, as if by remote. His big toe, supple and fleshy, linked directly to his head. The ball of his foot was like a pincushion. Lovingly, she circled the skin carved deep with lines that came from covering so much territory—airport walkways, rental car accelerators, and global office visits. But his instep was the most sensitive part. She eased her finger into the curve and pressed it with her thumb. Then curling up her hand, Lexi rolled the inner arch with her knuckles. David's cock hardened, and he let out a laugh. Working deeper with both thumbs in the ball of his foot, she released the last bit of tension.

"Come up here," David called.

Lexi moved upward as though she were climbing a mountain, clenching one leg, then the other with her open palm.

Nearing the top, she laughed when he grabbed the hair on her crown.

"Guess we'll always be Tarzan and Jane, huh?" she said.

"You got it," he said in husky tones.

Then he pulled her up to him and, in one motion, rolled her over. Feverishly, he kissed her temple, then her neck, thumbing her nipples to a stand. Lexi moaned like a teenager in the midst of her awakening. In the throes of passion, Lexi felt as though David was touching her for the first time. She was ecstatic.

Lexi's desire peaked with nothing more than the briefest foreplay and she started to come when David tapped on her labia. Wetter than she'd been in weeks, she was ready to surrender, just as they began.

Lexi screamed as David moved through her. Not because it hurt. Or because she was surprised. But because it was more precious than any lovemaking that had come before. Overpowered by delicate sounds and the beauty of their bodies rocking gently like waves against a pebbly shore, she felt the tears run down her cheeks as her orgasms broke. She imagined herself as a celestial bird. Perhaps she'd become the red-tailed hawk, the one Native Americans believed carried messages to God.

"Slowly," she whispered, as he prolonged her spasms.

Then like waves on a Grecian urn, immortalized as they moved toward their crested peak, their bodies stilled. Hovering like gentle doves, they locked together.

When the spell broke, Lexi whispered, "May God bless us."

"He has, Lexi. Over and over. Please, don't forget that. No matter what."

"Okay. You're right. But I want us to be safe."

"We are safe."

"You're so strong, David."

"Because of you, darling."

Lexi awakened in the morning, feeling sad. As she stretched and flexed her feet, her thoughts turned bittersweet. Not knowing what would happen next, she took solace in the knowledge that she and David shared a love that would feed her throughout her life. Feeling blessed, she knew she'd always believed that lasting love was possible, having seen that kind of attachment between her parents. She and David were also a good team. Together, they'd do whatever they needed to do to meet the illness head on.

She went to her office and started her daily journaling. Her thoughts raced, and her pen moved fluidly to capture them. Starting with David's illness, her stream of consciousness touched on Rob and his young family, his boyhood, how devoted David had been to him. Then anger rose up inside her and her hand stopped moving. By releasing emotions, she typically let her heart outpace her head. But not today. Lexi started to trembled, then used every ounce of discipline to keep going. To feel—all at once—in her heart, her body, and yes, her soul, the tragic twist her life might take was overwhelming. Last night she'd been there for David. Today she needed to be here for herself. Did she dare to go deeper?

Could writing alone prevent her soft whimpers from turning into sobs, sobs that might awaken David, still asleep two doors down? She stopped to breathe deeply. The repetition soothed her. Soon she could feel the part of her that always was. The part she knew when she was still, or at peace. And it was always the same, no matter if she pictured herself as a nine-year-old, or at twenty-four or thirty-nine. Now, she felt it again. Today it felt divine, better than before. Or was that because at fifty-seven she was both more self-loving and more accustomed to being in the presence of her soul?

No matter what happened next, her love for David had taken a new turn. It was as though she imagined herself sinking and rising in the same moment. More powerful and more sobering than the prospect of death, the new sensation pulled her down like an inexorable force. It felt as though she were hurtling toward the middle of the earth. In the grip of fear, her spirit rose, and a lightness took hold. She sensed another way of being. A sense of something larger and kinder than the self she knew at fifty-seven stirred inside her and moved her forward. Outside her study, the wind picked up, and as the fall leaves, tossed from the ground, whirled by her window, she knew she was being moved by spirit

She could hear David in the hall, and put her pen down. He'd be heading to catch the 6:34 A.M. train. Maybe she'd just stay still. Better to send him off today on last night's wings of love, than risk showing him a sad but tender smile. Perhaps her eyes would water or, she'd break out in tears. Or had the tears gone straight through her pen, then mixed with the ink, and come out as healing words?

Perhaps she'd wait a bit longer and let her new words teach her how to love him now. She knew from the sensations in her breast and, nearby, in her heart that she was changing yet another time. That she and David would be more not less. Lexi sat back in her chair and rocked, watching for more leaves to blow by her window. But the branches were still, and the tree looked more beautiful than ever. The only leaves she could see were clustered around the trunk, like a soft bed. She could hear David's car in the driveway.

She sat still for a few moments, then rose from her desk to fix a pot of coffee. She'd been working on financial matters this week, and needed to make more progress. She'd start by calling Amanda and setting up an appointment. Amanda, one of her son's oldest friends, was working with a top headhunting firm, and could give her a good overview of the current job market. She'd tried Hank Effinger, her buddy from her days at Bradford Communications, who had his own placement firm, but he was out of town this week. He'd be able to help her zero in on the right job when the time came.

Having taken the first and biggest step, Lexi phoned Shakti to see if they might meet for lunch. Shakti, sensing the urgency in her voice, cancelled a meeting, and they agreed to meet at Armando's.

Playing a Miles Davis CD as she drove into Boston, Lexi could feel her mood spiral downward. Today the ragged tones of his trumpet had a wrenching effect on her. She felt so alone and raw. As she parked her car, her despair rippled through her like water, trapped and searching for a way out.

Lexi tripped on the last step going down to Armando's, but it wasn't until she saw Shakti that fear overpowered her.

Pulling out the chair at the table, she shouted, "I can be sued for every last dollar by your firm. And you never warned me."

"I always thought you knew about the investment."

"Then you knew."

"There are lots of deals like this. How could I have known *you* didn't know?"

"It's true, we never talk about investments," Lexi said.

"We could."

"I'm too upset now."

"Then do what you've always done. Hold the pain and the joy together. Things will start to feel different," Shakti said.

Lexi's eyes teared. "I can feel the pain."

"Place your hand on your heart. Your lotus heart."

Blinking back her tears, Lexi put her hand over her heart.

"*Parásiva*."

"The soul's journey?"

"You remember." Shakti smiled. "Yes."

"I'm too sad."

"Lexi, that's the part of your life that no one can ever take away. Let it feed you."

Lexi broke into tears. Unable to move beyond the fear, she forgave herself. Somehow she would pull together her conflicting emotions and move forward. She needed time to go deeper.

The next day Lexi met with Amanda. Hoping to keep herself on an even plane, she thought of the upcoming conversation as an exploration. She had plenty of time to decide whether or not to take a full-time job. Right now there was no need for another job, but it felt good to learn about the options.

"I was so happy you called me, Mrs. Morgan. I'm flattered that you asked me to help you."

"Please, call me Lexi."

"Okay. And I understand that you need to build a secure future. I'll go through all the positions we have, but I have a hunch that the perfect job for you just came in, right after you phoned. It's a dot-com firm, and they need someone right away."

"Amanda, I'm interested in exploring all the possibilities."

"I understand. But I hope you'll make time to talk with them. Trust me."

"I do."

"I know you must remember all those things about me. How

I took the car out before I got my license. And the accident."

"You're a lovely, capable woman, Amanda."

"Or that course I was getting a D in. Rob always told people how I got the teacher to agree to that double or nothing bet. How he used my grade on the next paper as my grade for the course. Then got fired."

"There were other reasons. I believe he resigned."

"That was after having sex with the freshman."

"Yes. You're right."

"But I *know* you, and even though I have only been doing professional searches for two years, this is a top firm and I'm a quick study."

"I hope I didn't mislead you when I talked about thinking big. And about equity. Income is important, too."

"Yes, I know. But it's not easy, Mrs. Morgan, when you want it all."

"Lexi."

"Yes. And what I have to say is difficult."

"I don't mind."

"No. I'll just say it. In this firm, we believe that one of the biggest problems in management is teamwork."

Lexi gave her a blank look.

"Most firms have gotten lost in process. America needs more entrepreneurship, and that means finding people who aren't afraid to, you know, kick ass."

Lexi laughed.

"Really, you know what I mean. Take charge, Mrs. M—, I mean Lexi. Do you know that over five percent of people in the service industry are employed solely to say 'I'm sorry?' We've not only gotten used to screw-ups, we plan on them."

"Could I *tap* ass?"

"*Knee* ass. Remember when you had that haunted house for

Rob and *made* us feel those gross eyeballs and brains? Then you jumped out of the closet and scared the shit out of us?"

"It was just for fun. Really. But I'm a lot older."

"Lexi, you'll lose the best jobs if you think that way. You go in there and take charge. America needs it. And they'll pay *big* for someone who's not a wimp. Someone who can prevent all those mistakes. They'll cut you a lot of slack because you're fun, too. Remember, fun. That's our firm's mantra."

"I need to gradually build and maintain a stable income, Amanda. My husband is ill."

"I'm sorry, Lexi. I did talk with Rob after you called. And I don't want to be rude, but you don't have *time* to work your way up. With this group you'll be starting near the top. And the key is moving *fast*. We believe that a great idea plus fun equals a million-dollar business with well-paid executives."

"Well."

"No, really. This is all new. This job market sucks. You have to stand out. Establish your talent."

"Not just do things for other people?"

"Right."

"It's been a long time since I thought about myself first."

"That's okay. It's all about what you want to give. The part of you that's special. The part the world needs."

"I like that. But isn't a dot-com business too big a risk?"

"If dot-coms are ever going to come back, it will be for three reasons: they'll feature products that don't exist in any other form: they'll be cost-effective, and each hugely successful company will have learned how to generate a megabillion idea plus the infrastructure to support it."

"So, what, specifically, is the job?"

"Trust me, Lexi. It's a blockbuster idea. They'll describe it better than I can."

"So, I just say I can knee ass."

"Talk about strategy. They don't know anything about it. Or marketing."

"Amanda," said Lexi, alarmed by what she was hearing, "I appreciate your enthusiasm, but I need *money*. They don't sound . . ."

"And they need *you*, strategy, and marketing. The sky's the limit."

"Oh, Amanda . . ."

"Don't do anything you don't want to do."

"Okay."

"I'll have Wanda call them right now to tell them you're coming. How's tomorrow?"

"Why not?" said Lexi, bemused.

"Then let's talk in detail about your professional background, and the other types of jobs and industries that would be a good fit. We're very thorough."

Lexi was thankful to go on Amanda's mystery interview the next day. It took her mind off David, and there was nothing more to learn until they met again with the doctor next week. The interview would be a good warm-up for her job search. When Hank Effinger returned from vacation, she'd see if he had some other ideas for her. What did she have to lose?

As Lexi pulled on her pantyhose, she thought about how much her life had changed since she first started working at home. She could wear what she wanted, and it almost never included slipping into a skirt. Having clients in the arts felt good. They wore casual but interesting clothes, and so did she. Although she'd be talking with a young dot-com owner, Lexi knew it was still an interview. She probably wouldn't wear a skirt, but the pantyhose firmed her up. And anyway, what did a take-charge woman wear these days? A pinstriped, black

Armani pantsuit, with some chunky silver, ass-kicking jewelry, looked just right.

She was to meet with Amber Jentes, one of the owners of Only For You. As Lexi waited in the reception area, she looked through a small display of the company's brochures, picking one with vibrant reds, pinks and oranges. The slick brochure with an accordion fold described a number of Web sites. Wondering which might be the most profitable, Lexi's eyes stopped at the site featured in the center of the brochure: www.cybersexier. No wonder Amanda hadn't said much. Well, at least she could entertain David with the story. Rob would probably wonder why Lexi thought Amanda had changed.

Composed, Lexi smiled broadly as she shook hands with Amber Jentes, noting with interest her pierced nose and well cut, purplish hair. She looked about twenty-three, and underplayed her affluence and femininity. Amber's bright eyes were personable and Lexi liked the natural way Amber sat in her executive chair, neither stiff nor sloppy.

"No, actually my partner and I liked the fact that you're . . . you know . . . have done so many things. It makes us . . . ah . . . more credible."

"So, you want to shift your business mix?" Lexi asked.

"Well, there's a lot of competition right now. Alan's parents have been funding us, and . . ."

"You have investors?"

"Well, they said that if we did something that really helped people . . ."

"Like counseling? Over the Internet, at all times of the day?"

"Yes. You'd actually be able to see the therapist, all of his or her reactions . . . but nobody would see you."

"Patients would be anonymous."

"Of course, we wouldn't allow any abuse."

"No, no. Of course not."

"And it would be a way for sex therapists to boost their income. Work whenever they wanted."

"Even from home."

"With this technology, even the car."

"A completely new product, really."

"Yes. Our research shows people are usually embarrassed. But they'd like this."

"And of course, there's no need . . ."

"Not with this. And we could give you equity in the company. Your experience is valuable to us. We know about your work with Bradford Communications, and your focus on strategy and marketing."

Lexi was electric. "Amber, I'm intrigued. You've peaked my imagination. Sex has been the crazy glue in my own life. I know there's a huge market of people who'd like to broaden the way they think about sex. The key is thinking through who your customers are."

"That's right."

"The only way to protect a great idea is to do it better than anyone else."

"Lexi, I'll tell Ted and Alan about our talk. But what do you think our greatest challenge is?"

"When you have a great idea, competitors will flock to it. The first company to establish a strong business base typically wins. We need to have everything in order before we launch and roll out this service. That's the best way to defend against counterattacks. Just do it better from the start. That requires a huge investment of time and imagination."

"That's the kind of planning that Amanda says you've been doing for years."

"Yes."

"Wow."

"Yes."

In just one week, David had linked up with one of the top oncology surgeons at Mass General. His team took David and Lexi through a preview of the surgery and the decisions that would have to wait until the surgeon opened David's lung. Rob and his wife, Lydia, and Allison stopped by the hospital the night before the operation. The toddler's antics chased the fear out of the room. When it was time to leave, Rob held his father for a long time.

Once David was in the recovery room, Lexi called Rob and reached his voice mail. She didn't have much to say—little to leave as a message.

She caught Lydia at her office. "The doctor just called. We'd expected about a two-hour operation. And it was three and a half hours."

"What did they find?"

"Two tumors. They removed one lobe of the lung. But I won't know anything else until tomorrow."

"That seems like such a long time."

"I'll be staying here tonight. I'll phone you after we see the doctor."

"God bless you, Lexi."

"Thank you. Take care, Lydia. Love to you and Rob."

Lexi decided to call Shakti.

"It's not good, Shakti. The surgery was extensive."

"I'm sorry."

"I'll call you tomorrow, when I know more," Lexi said, enervated. "I'm going to see the nurse now."

I'm holding you both in my prayers."

"Thank you. It feels good."

Lexi woke with a start and tried to make sense of her surroundings when the beeping started. After a night of constant interruptions, the regularity of the beeps created an odd rhythm. But she was groggy from sleeping on and off through the night. Lying sideways on the grey blue vinyl chair, Lexi stretched her long legs over the footrest, but there was precious little to support her neck.

David's eyes flickered as the beeps continued. Lexi reached over to touch him. She located the call button clipped to the metal bar around his bed and pressed down hard with her other hand.

"Good morning, darling," she said.

"Hi," he said, as though mustering all of his energy for the final sprint in a biker's marathon.

"You did real well, sweetheart."

"Oh, yeah."

"Yep. Dr. Raub is pleased. He'll be in to talk with us this morning. Soon, in fact," she said, looking up at the wall clock.

April, the night nurse, responded to her call.

"It's one of the tubes. Could it be the pain medication?"

"It's empty. I'll get another," April said briskly.

Lexi took in a deep breath to center herself, then looked back at David. "Bet you're sore."

"I don't know what I am. Just bloody uncomfortable."

The door opened again, letting in more cacophonous noises from the hall. Lexi was growing used to the odd, industrial sounds of equipment being rolled down the corridors, amid the din of muffled voices. An attendant clanked a brown plastic tray on the narrow table stretched over David's bed, eager to retreat from the room just as fast as he'd entered it.

"Breakfast?" Lexi asked.

"Eat what you can. The doctor ordered extra liquids."

"How am I, Lexi?" David asked, unaware of the commotion.

"You were a bit uncomfortable last night. You'll feel better after the anesthesia wears off. There's pain medication in the I.V."

"The surgery, Lexi."

Softening her eyes, she said, "They removed two tumors, David. And two-thirds of one lung," she added. After a pause, she continued, "That's not unusual, Dr. Raub says. He'll know more today."

David closed his eyes, and his uncommitted mouth stayed still as he slipped back into a nap.

Reaching for a straw, Lexi pulled off the paper and placed it in the plastic cup, ready to give him a sip when he opened his eyes.

David came home six days later. With the help of the home care services, he made good progress. Every day he seemed to grow stronger. Bedside chats gave structure to the days.

Lexi found strength through prayer and meditation, and eased into a special rhythm as she cared for David. Intimate moments had new beauty. Drawing a warm washcloth down David's arm, Lexi could tell by the light in his eyes when he was about to say something funny. Standing at his side, as she combed Rob's gel through his hair, she liked how she could see down the fresh furrows of his thinning auburn hair. And when she leaned over to kiss him, she smelled the skin that, even in darkness, would have drawn her to him.

About three weeks into his convalescence, David asked her to stay with him for a while after breakfast.

"I've been thinking about the loan against the house."

"Please don't. I'm fine."

"I need to."

"Okay."

"You can use the life insurance payment to clear the loan. The house has appreciated. Probably eighty percent. So, if you want to sell it, it would be more than a nest egg."

"I know, darling. You told me this before."

"My deferred compensation will provide a decent monthly income."

"I know. You've mentioned this."

"I want you to be comfortable, Lexi."

"Each day you're stronger, darling."

Despite the efforts of visiting nurses to help keep David's lungs clear, he developed an infection. The doctor insisted he be treated in the hospital. Lexi was concerned about the toll that being back in the hospital would take on his already frail body, and used a variety of relaxation techniques to quell his anxiety. Ministering to him each day, she learned which ones worked best.

"Sometimes the pain recedes."

"When we pray?"

"Maybe it's your voice."

"It's our way of being together."

"I love you, Lexi."

"I love you, darling. Now let's visualize all the colors of the spectrum again."

"Yes."

"Does it seem like it's the heat of the warmer colors on the band that holds them all together?"

"Hmm?"

"The yellow and oranges are hugging you now, just like the sun. Now the light's white."

"It feels like you."

"I'm linking up with your soul."

"I feel like myself now."

"Peaceful?"

"Yes."

"Good," Lexi whispered, with the heat rising in her hands as she stretched them over David's chest.

David napped on and off that afternoon. When he awakened, Lexi shared her news. The Prism Theater had committed to a full season of plays that explored the mysteries of the soul and the way people create meaning from intolerable pain. And they'd commissioned her to do another project. She would develop a marketing campaign around the concept.

"I'm thrilled because so many of my favorites are included. Remember when I saw Richard Burton in *Equus*?"

"With your parents?"

"Yes. When I was in graduate school. And *Master Class*, which we saw together."

"Passion and discipline. Wasn't that your favorite line?"

"Yes. You remembered."

"What other ones?"

"I suggested your favorite: *Amy's View*."

"You know, I'd like to see that again."

"Next season. So then, as if the new project wasn't enough, I've also taken a full-time job. But I can work from home."

"Oh, Lexi, I wish . . ."

"I'm thrilled about it. Really, I am. It's an established dot-com and they've given me a generous equity position to start, with more later."

"Well, I hope they deserve you. What's the business?"

"They help people build their potential."

"Oh, like positive-thinking gurus?"

"Yes, actually."

"You'll be good at that."

"You rest now, darling."

Back home that night, Lexi tensed when the doorbell rang. She'd invited Rob and Lydia to dinner. Having been alone so much lately, she had wanted company, but now that they were here, she wondered if it would have been better just to stay quiet and relax. She relaxed her shoulders as she gripped the doorknob, letting some of her tension flow into the brass knob.

When she saw Rob's smile, all of her anxiety slipped away. The spark from his warm, brown eyes, lured her into a peaceful place. And Lydia was a jewel in Lexi's life. Lexi thought of her daughter-in-law as the compensation she finally got for not having a daughter of her own.

Closing the door behind him, Rob said with concern, "We stopped by to see Dad. He looks tired. He was sleeping but woke up for a minute just before we left. I was sort of sorry we disturbed him."

"Yes. He's so thin. And his skin is gray now," Lexi said softly, as she steadied herself.

"His eyes brightened when he saw us, though," Lydia said, as she moved into the hallway.

Nodding, Lexi said, "He's still reaching out, so keep visiting him. He likes company."

"How are you?" Lydia asked. She put her arms around Lexi.

Lexi's eyes watered and she whispered, "I'm okay."

Rob moved in close and gave her a bear hug, lifting her off the ground.

"I'm so glad you're both here," Lexi sighed. Ushering them in, she added, "The dinner is as simple as promised, but we'll eat in the library. I've been doing that lately. It's cozy."

They headed into the kitchen together, the site of so many upbeat family gatherings. Lexi had everything organized, as usual. Rob headed toward the tray filled with water and wine glasses. Picking up the pneumatic corkscrew, lying next to the ice bucket and tongs, he opened the bottle of burgundy his mother had chosen for the occasion.

"I've picked up some things we can heat up. Things the microwave won't hurt too much," Lexi said unapologetically, pointing to two containers filled with duck breasts and wild rice.

"I did bake some acorn squash, though. That's always been comfort food for me. I'll take it out when everything else is ready."

Lydia started to microwave the main parts of the meal, while Lexi added her homemade raspberry vinaigrette dressing to the arugala salad, tossing in some cherry tomatoes and fresh basil.

Lydia arranged the dinner on square, cream colored plates made by a ceramist in Northern California. The simplicity of just being with her children made Lexi feel grounded. She used her favorite handwrought brass and iron serving utensils, shaped like branches on a tree, to serve the salad greens into three deep black bowls.

Hot from the oven, the acorn squash was as vibrant as the autumn leaves. Sniffing the cinnamon, Lexi watched the butter swish from one side of the squash's caramel-colored center to the other, and placed a piece carefully on each dinner plate.

Lydia picked up a tray and led the way through the glass doors to the library. "I love the mums, Lexi," she said, looking at the potted plants tucked into a big basket on the octagonal mahogany table. "Mixed together, the rust, amber, and brown colors almost look like an open field. And they're so soft."

"Yes. They're round and fuzzy, aren't they?" Lexi said and she heard the lack of energy in her own voice. Her mood took a sudden nosedive as she felt the absence of David at the table.

Picking up on her mother-in-law's feelings, Lydia changed the pace. "I was thinking about you today, Lexi. You've been such an inspiration to us since David became ill. It's hard to be down about it, because you keep smiling and carrying on as though everything was business as usual."

"That's very kind, Lydia. Keeping myself going is like medicine," Lexi said haltingly.

"Is that what feeds your spirit?" Lydia asked, hoping to draw Lexi out.

"In many ways it does," Lexi said.

Proceeding in animated tones, Lydia said, "Lexi, where did you get it? You emanate joy. I want to do that for Allison. It's a kind of energy, isn't it?"

Relaxing, Lexi said, "It might sound odd, but I first became aware of how important high spirits are from riding horses. When I was young, I would dream about them constantly. In fact, my first recurring dream was about horses."

"Do you feel like sharing it?" Lydia asked, sensing that she'd hit on something.

Lexi knew Lydia was trying to keep her energy up, and she was warmed by it.

"Sure. I'll try," she said. "When I was about ten years old, I started to dream about mustangs. I dreamt that I'd see a group of them off in the distance. Always, whenever I would just about reach them, they would gallop off.

"Alone in my bed, I dreamed the same dream many times. And each time I felt the excitement in my body. The power and speed of the horses triggered new sensations in me. Soon I felt as strong and beautiful as the horses. It was as though I kept jumping higher, as if to catch something airborne—something invisible."

"That's so beautiful, Lexi. It's really you," Lydia said with enormous enthusiasm.

"But, I wanted a piece of that spirit. I decided to become it. Live it. And now when I see a horse, even in one of those hokey car commercials, I feel a rush."

"That's beautiful."

"I feel blessed, but nothing's that simple. There's always the chance that we'll lose what's most precious," she said, as her voice trembled. Then, finding her words, she started again slowly. "There's a part of me that will die when David dies. The part of me that merged with him so long ago. I get sad when I think about it. But, there's another part. One he always supported. And that's my spirit. And at some point," she said as her voice quivered, "if David dies, I'll pull through it, and my spirit will move me on."

Lydia stood and began clearing the dinner dishes. She paused at the entry to the kitchen, balancing the dishes like a pro. Lexi knew that Lydia had once dreamed of having a career in the theater. She'd spent a year in Manhattan waiting for a break and then she met Rob.

"You're beautiful, Lexi. Inside and out."

Lexi felt herself flush and didn't quite know how to respond. "Like jazz?" she asked, surprising herself.

"Like Louis Armstrong's arrangements," Rob said. "People say he was like an angel."

The serious mood disappeared. Dessert was coconut cake with a white chocolate cream center. By the end of the evening, all three of them were satiated.

Lexi began sleeping regularly at the hospital. Although she had a small cot in David's room, she'd often tuck in beside David at night when the hospital routine was less intrusive. She'd hold him in her arms. She worried about the opaque finish of his eyes. He was often listless and sad.

After two weeks of watching David slip, Lexi said, "No more silence. Silence keeps everything the same."

David's pain medication had been reduced at his own urging, and he had a little more clarity.

"I'm scared," David said in a low voice.

"Of course. So much is uncertain."

"But there's more for us to do, to be." He was begging for more time.

"We've loved well, David. And once we learn to love deeply, we're always wanting more. It's the other side of the coin. Love is boundless."

"But, what did I do wrong?"

"Nothing. This is a natural process."

"And now what?"

"Put your faith in God. Ask for His will to be done. Or ask for something specific. To find peace."

"I have no major regrets. But I just wish I hadn't made so many mistakes."

"This is how we figure out what matters."

"It is?"

"A mistake I made twenty-nine years ago has made all the difference."

"What are you thinking about?"

"Barbados."

"Ah."

"And if I hadn't been kicked into Eden, I wouldn't have found you."

"Then I love your mistakes."

"Remember when I started that kitchen fire in the rental house in Boca Grande? And how word got out? And no one would rent to us after that?"

"Oh, Jesus," he said trying to laugh. "All these years there was so much to figure out. Now, I'm letting go."

Tears streaming down her face, Lexi said, "That's good."

"It's miraculous."

"Part of something bigger."

"With you in the very center of my heart," he said, gripping her hand.

"Your heart feels so vast," she said as she leaned over and massaged his chest with her other hand.

"I feel safe."

"And you're filled with love."

"It feels good."

"It's enough, isn't it?"

"Yes."

⌒

A week later Lexi and Rob talked with the doctors. The cancer had nearly run its course. No further surgery or treatments were in order. David had signed the DNR agreement before the surgery, stipulating that he not be attached to a life-support system.

David's doctor believed that David would die within the month. All they could do now was help manage the pain. After talking with David, Lexi and Rob agreed that he would be more comfortable at home.

Taking David home for the last time, Lexi prayed for help. She asked for the strength to do everything necessary to bring him peace. And to carry on with grace and dignity.

Each day Lexi selected music to soothe and comfort him as he slept on and off. During the hours when he was less sedated, Lexi ran videos of old favorites from the TV in the armoire. *Breakfast at Tiffany's, It Happened One Night, Like Water for Chocolate* and *African Queen*. Friends would come and go.

Despite the help of three medications, David's nausea worsened. He grew thinner, his skin had the folds of a newborn calf. Often too weak to walk, even with assistance, he was catheterized by the nurse, who came each day to check his vital signs and, periodically, draw blood.

At night, Lexi played Gregorian chants. After lighting the

candles in the room, she'd snuggle in bed with David. Just lying together and holding hands brought her world back together after a full day of caregiving.

One afternoon, when Lexi sensed David was drifting away from her, she called Rob suggesting that he, Lydia and Allison stop by that evening. She did not indicate that David was in critical condition. It wasn't her way. They would suffer enough pain when David was gone. She telephoned the minister who had been their pastor since the first days of their marriage. To him she confided the situation. David was dying. The minister would be there with them.

Once everyone was together, they surrounded David in a circle, holding hands as he lay in bed. Reverend Bowen guided them in a blessing. Talking softly about things David had done to make the world a better place, he relieved him of any other duties. And when the Reverend spoke of God's eternal love and a lush resting place, David's eyes opened. For a moment, his opaque gaze vanished. Like the soul reaching out to embrace loved ones, David's eyes glowed.

Then the Reverend read. Lexi, seated between Allison and David, prayed for strength. The Reverend read from Ecclesiastes: *"For everything there is a season, and a time for every matter under heaven."* Lexi's eyes teared as the rich tones of his voice reverberated in her chest. Allison gurgled and made a sound in an attempt to convey whatever was on her young, innocent mind. *"A time to be born, and a time to die."* Lexi squeezed Allison's little hand and winked as he read. *"A time to plant, and a time to pluck what is planted."* She wondered if Lydia might bring Allison over to work with Lexi in the garden over the summer. Maybe even help next weekend. Her musing helped her gain courage. The Reverend concluded. *"A time for war, and a time for peace."*

Touched by the blessing, Lexi felt serene, even after Rob,

196 • *Holly Hayes*

Lydia, and Allison left the house. Her body had slowed to a murmur during the afternoon, the day she knew would be David's last. As her eyes lingered on David's weary face, she smelled a sweetness crowding out the noxious odor of a sick room. Sweeter than honeysuckle, softer than lilac. The scent lifted her spirit. Lexi felt blessed, knowing she would be alone with David when he died.

Lexi, still dressed in her soft jersey pants and knit top, slid into bed next to David, wrapping one arm over his shoulder. Cheek to cheek and thighs pressed together, they rested. Effortlessly, her chest rose with his, followed by a slow release of air. Again. And again. As the moments passed, Lexi, feeling no more than the warmth of their bodies, was at peace.

David's muffled cough awakened her. Looking over at the antique Oriental birdcage, high on a carved ebony stand to the right of the armoire, Lexi's eyes lingered on the beauty of the open space. There was nothing inside the delicately curved wooden slats that gave shape to the cage, except two circular jade rings where the birds once rested, and two blue and white porcelain birdseed pots. Yet the empty birdcage's beauty sustained her. A favorite possession for over fifteen years, it was an unsung poem. Sacred, as it waited for whatever birds had flown away or might be there in the future.

For Lexi, David, lying at her side, would always be the man who resided in the circle of her core—complete and vital. Thinking of Michelangelo's pen and ink drawing, she held his hand and knew that they'd merged for the last time.

Something was changing, and her heart slowed to monitor the shift. David's pulse was weak.

Lexi nibbled softly at his ear, then whispered, "Thank you, darling." Slowly, she said, "You gave me everything I needed. And I imagine us intertwined forever. Not just our bodies, the way they are now. But our souls. That, alone, will keep me whole. I know I'll be fine."

Focusing all of her energy, Lexi encased David in an imaginary beam of white light and said, "Safe journey, darling. I love you and always will."

As Lexi's body began to quiver, she felt a huge release. David was gone. And the room filled with a wild energy. His spirit unleashed. And she bathed in it.

Then whirring like a golden orb, she stilled herself. Lexi felt like a hummingbird. Moving in a circle-eight pattern, she was pure vibration. Alone and whole.

WITH THANKS

To my mother, Caroline Drick, whose love of life and dedication to family have inspired mine.

To Carl, David, Pookie, Ken, and Matt for their loving presence.

To Sonia Choquette and Sandi Gelles-Cole, without whose encouragement I might not have written and without whose wisdom I would not have succeeded.

To Robert Bosnak, Janice O'Rourke, Penny Rieck, and Allen Schoer who made me more than I was.

To Holly Badgley, Libby Bishop, Niki Bryan, Pat Burns, Nilda Carlo, Maria Carter, Kara Cook, Terry Daugirdas, Carol Doumani, George and Eriko Drick, Joan Ebzery, Mary Kay Fry, Chris Gilson, Rebecca Hall, Rita and Tom Herskovits, Jill Isselhard, Sylvia Lavietes, Chase Levey, Tina Lieberman, Judy Marcus, Sue Marineau, Pat Moffat, Connie Moskow, Carolyn Nahrwold, Mim Neal, Cheryl Perlitz, Alyssa Rapp, Gerry and Michael Silverstein, Marjorie Stern, Peter Stern, Marilynn Thoma, Joel Weiner, Pam Wilson, and B. Wu whose honesty and support hastened my progress.

To Bob Allen, Ruth Berger, Maria Ballantyne, Mark Victor Hansen, Lynda Knott, Marshall Thurber, Mary Jo Zazueta, and Bei Min Zhang who always moved me forward.

And, to the memory of my father, a quiet hero.

Threads of Passion may be purchased
through your local bookstore,
on Amazon.com,
or by telephoning 1-800-247-6553.